The Old Black Curtain

By CJ Paxton

FriesenPress

Suite 300 - 990 Fort St
Victoria, BC, V8V 3K2
Canada

www.friesenpress.com

Copyright © 2020 by CJ Paxton
First Edition — 2020

All rights reserved.

No part of this publication may be reproduced in any form, or by any means, electronic or mechanical, including photocopying, recording, or any information browsing, storage, or retrieval system, without permission in writing from FriesenPress.

ISBN
978-1-5255-6250-1 (Hardcover)
978-1-5255-6251-8 (Paperback)
978-1-5255-6252-5 (eBook)

Fiction, Romance

Distributed to the trade by The Ingram Book Company

PROLOGUE

Deep Breath

THE BUS WAS warm as it continued down the trans-Canada highway. She thanked God it wasn't too crowded as she sat at the back with her head down and the oversized jacket bunched up around her. She shifted uncomfortably in her seat, pressing a hand over her still broken ribs. The ball cap was hiding her bruised face and keeping her book slightly higher in her hand prevented any of the other passengers from engaging her. Taking another deep breath, she was careful not to aggravate her injuries further. She hoped her next destination would be safer, and that for once she could stay quietly hidden away.

CHAPTER ONE

The Request

... Eighteen months earlier

THE RAIN WAS coming down hard, harder than it had been all week. Ordinarily, I enjoyed the rain, but today, today I was in no mood for it. I was sitting in a stuffy conference room with my older brother Thomas Murphy, one of the top divorce attorneys currently in London, England. Seated across from us, a tad too close to each other for my liking, was my soon to be ex-wife Robin, and her attorney, Mr. Edward Barnes. The thought of them together surged through my mind and I wondered, *was he her lover?* From the beginning of our marriage, I could sense something was amiss, the late nights and long weekends with 'friends'. I suspected she might be seeing someone, but I never thought it was her divorce attorney.

Sixteen years ago when I first met Robin, she was the most beautiful woman I had ever seen. Tall and slim, with long blond hair and ocean blue eyes, at the time she was everything I thought I wanted. A natural wordsmith who could talk anyone into just about anything and she played me, so very well. The truth of the matter is that Robin stayed married to me just long enough to receive the largest sum based on our prenuptial agreement — three and a half million. Now, to me three and a half million isn't exactly life-altering and I wasn't concerned about paying her out, but I wasn't thrilled with the idea of losing it, either.

At eighteen, I decided to do my higher education abroad. I applied to the University of Edinburgh and was accepted into their four-year Computer Science program. During the final year, along with my mate Hamish MacPhail, we created the world's leading security software called Obscure Security Coverage or OSC for short. About a month before we graduated, Hamish and I were approached about selling OSC. One night down at the pub having a few pints, Hamish laid out his whole vision of us running our own computer company and becoming the world's leading software duo. He is definitely the dreamer between us. Personally, I was on the fence, knowing I could do anything I wanted. I thought of staying in university and working towards my PhD. Hamish suggested I do just that while he built up the business. He had already received his business degree, and I had all the capital we would need to get started. Needless to say, after a few days Hamish wore me down and I agreed to his plan.

So Hamish and I declined the offer on OSC and built M&M Tech instead. Being the people person between us, Hamish took care of the day-to-day running of things. Business was not my strong suit so I mainly tinkered on our latest projects, improving OSC and rolling out the newest versions of everything while working on my PhD. After three years, we expanded into online tech support and services. Our stock was rising and Hamish and I began making a name for ourselves.

When my father passed away, Thomas and I inherited everything. Our father had been the top attorney in Toronto and unsurprisingly had built up quite the nest egg. With Hamish and me doing fine with M&M Tech and inheriting half a fortune, I was doing rather well financially. So I really can't say that I minded giving Robin the sum.

What I did mind were the last fifteen years she spent convincing me we were happy. The lies were bad enough, but worse than that, I fell for them and didn't notice. I thought I was happy, I thought we were happy. I mean, our marriage wasn't perfect and we certainly had our problems but still, I thought we were at least content. Now, even after I learned of the affairs and knew she no longer wanted to be with me, I couldn't bring myself to leave her. I had made a vow, given my word, and I don't break my word. I had made it clear from the start, if Robin wanted out of our marriage, she'd have to be the one to file for it. And she did.

Now the four of us were sitting in Mr. Barnes' stuffy conference room, watching Robin get everything she wanted, my money, her freedom, even my flat. Though I was sad to part with it — it was a great flat —Thomas convinced me it would be better in the long run. A clean and simple divorce would be best all around. It wasn't worth fighting over a flat, no matter how amazing, when I could simply go and buy a new one, so I relented. We all signed the papers, and now we just had to wait thirty days and our divorce would be finalized. A huge part of my life had just ended, and I was completely unprepared for where life was about to take me.

"And, finished," Thomas said as he put the cap back on his pen. He looked over to me, pleased with a job well done. With the papers signed, Thomas and I stood from the large conference table and headed towards the door.

"Michael…" I heard Robin say.

I turned to face her, expecting more, but there was nothing, just a soft smile and a nod. I nodded back, then turned to leave with Thomas following behind.

We left Robin to her spoils and to her Mr. Barnes and went to the elevator. Just as Thomas pressed the button for the door, my cell went off. The call was short but impactful, and I was at a loss for words. I took a sharp breath to settle myself as I hung up and pocketed my phone. Once inside the elevator, I turned to Thomas to let him know what had happened.

"That, ahh… that was Mr. King, our aunts' attorney… he's in town and needs to see us. It's Betty and Ronnie," I started, but was struggling to get my words out so I tried again, "Betty and Ronnie have… have passed away." My voice broke as I said the words. I quickly wiped a small tear from my eye as I let Thomas take in the news. He remained silent. I couldn't tell what he was thinking.

"He would like to see us tomorrow morning at your office. Go over their wills. Around 10 am." Thomas nodded as the elevator doors opened into the parking garage and we stepped out. He ran his hands over his face, reeling from the painful news. Thomas and I had never agreed on much, but we loved our aunts. They raised us.

"Fuck this. I need a drink. How 'bout a pint down at the pub?" Thomas said after a few moments.

"No thanks," I told him, shaking my head, "think I'll just... I'm just gonna walk for a bit. I'll see you later." I turned from Thomas, heading towards the sidewalk. I could barely hear Thomas ask me if I was sure over the rain, the distance growing between us with each step I took, so I just gave a wave behind me and kept walking. My mind was officially on overdrive and I needed space to calm down and refocus.

I found that walking the busy streets always managed to make me feel better, especially at night when the evening fog rolled in. This night, however, it wasn't working, not with the pains of this day. Divorcing Robin and losing my aunts all at once was simply too much. The only person I had left in the world was Thomas, and though I loved my brother, that thought didn't fill me with much comfort. Thomas had been supportive during my divorce, representing me and putting me up in his spare room. But I knew Thomas too well. Though he might mean well at times, he always does what's best for himself first. A pint might ease his grief but it wouldn't do much for mine.

By the time I got back to Thomas' place, it was well past midnight. He had already turned in for the night, but in spite of my exhaustion, I was too wound up to sleep. I got myself a glass and grabbed the first bottle from Thomas's bar that my hand touched, then moved to the couch and poured myself a sizable drink. I read the bottle: Spirit of Dublin Teeling Whiskey Single Malt, aged thirty years. The bottle had to be worth nearly €1,600. Thomas always did have expensive taste. I downed his over-priced whiskey then poured another, and another, and another. While drowning my grief, I noticed how my brother's OCD characterized his home. Everything was neat and in its place. His whole flat looked as though he had cut it out directly from a magazine.

Thomas' flat was almost a mirror image of himself, pristine and orderly. Between the two of us, Thomas was the handsome 'put together' one. Tall and muscular with short brown hair neatly kept in place, the grey just starting to show along his temple, and blue eyes and a soft smile he used to make women swoon. He was always clean-shaven and dressed for business. Thomas and I looked similar in some ways but there were definite differences. For starters, I'm three years younger. Thomas, Hamish and I had actually celebrated my 42nd birthday three days before Robin and I signed our divorce papers. I felt as though I was off to a rough start. I'm 5'7" to his 5'11", slender to his muscular frame, but I'm not without definition. My short curly hair, that is now practically all silver and grey throughout, always looked unkempt. My eyes, a soft green-blue enhanced by my black full-framed glasses. My smile, though surrounded by a short scruffy beard, could be as soft and charming as Thomas's. I hardly ever kept myself clean-shaven. No, unlike Thomas, I had a more rugged look. I can pull off that clean cut look when necessary, but it just isn't me. Where Thomas constantly wears high-end tailored suits, I prefer my worn out jeans and button-down, collared shirts for the sake of comfort.

I poured myself another glass of whiskey and went over to the bookcase. Drink in hand, I bent down to the bottom shelf and pulled a photo album out before wandering back to the couch. After downing what I'd just poured I put the glass on the coffee table and opened the album. The first few pages were all of Thomas and me growing up in Toronto. We were a real family back then, or at least the illusion of a real family. However, all this was before our mother died.

She was heading to meet our father at a work function of his when a drunk driver hit her. We were told that she didn't suffer much, as she died on impact, but our lives were never the same. I was eight when this happened. Our father had his older twin sisters, Betty and Veronica (or Ronnie as she preferred) come and live with us so he could bury himself in work. He had never been an overly warm or affectionate man, but after mother died, any warmth left in him quickly vanished. Our father then spent the rest of his life making money, believing that was all he needed. Once Thomas passed the bar he went to work with our father at his firm Murphy's at Law, and they became the best in the city. Eventually Thomas convinced our father to expand the firm, bring on more clients and open up branches in the UK to start. He wasn't keen at first but eventually Thomas got his way. But despite our father's death, and business expansions, Thomas refused to let the business name falter; his clients would and could expect the same exceptional work they had always provided.

I poured myself another drink and continued to flip through the album. The next few pages were pictures of us as teenagers. At this point, we had moved away from our father who found his life much easier when we weren't around. We travelled with our aunts. Each picture was from a different place, a different town, a different country. Betty and Ronnie loved to travel and wanted to see the world, but the way we all travelled was a bit unorthodox. Our aunts were freelance consultants, and they travelled all over the world restructuring bookstores in decline. We would stay in each town until the store was once again turning a profit, and then move onto the next. Thomas and I would work in the shop part-time while being home-schooled by Ronnie. To be honest, I loved it. I must have tried to read every single book that we came across, but of course, never quite managed it. Thomas, on the other hand, hated every moment of it. He found it boring and would always run off with new friends he'd made, leaving me with all the work. Thomas was always more social than me. Of course, Betty and Ronnie's dream was to open their own bookstore one day, and they finally did a couple of years ago. Happily, they ran a tranquil little bookshop in a lovely little city, until they met their untimely deaths.

I turned the next couple of album pages showing Thomas graduating college and then my graduation. Pictures of my wedding with Robin followed. I drank another long nip of whiskey as I flipped through the pages of wedding photos wondering if she was already cheating on me then. Given how my life was going of late, it's possible I was becoming a cynic. I hated myself for looking so damn happy. As I examined the pictures I felt like burning them, but that could have been the whiskey. Either way, it was the last thought I remember having that night.

THE OLD BLACK CURTAIN

The next morning, I woke to the grating sound of Thomas in the kitchen, grinding coffee beans. I slowly sat myself up on the couch, still in my, now wrinkled, blue suit from the day before. Rubbing my temples, I prayed the obscenely loud sound of the coffee grinder would stop. The nearly empty bottle of whiskey and my dry, empty glass were sitting on the coffee table, the photo album lying open on the floor. My raging headache let me know I was awake.

"Morning," Thomas said once the grinder stopped, louder than he knew he needed to be. "You might want to get ready, we have the will reading at ten, remember." Thomas was already showered, shaved and ready to go for the day. I looked at my watch, it was only 8:30. I had time.

I left Thomas to his grinder and dragged myself into a hot shower. My head was throbbing from the half bottle of whiskey I had consumed but the hot water was helping. By the time I was showered and dressed in the only other suit I had with me, Thomas had finished making coffee and had a full tumbler waiting for me. I took my coffee with thanks as we headed out into the centre of London.

My intense hangover combined with the deaths and divorce put me in a rather irritable mood, not a good start to the day. With our father gone, Betty and Ronnie were the only family Thomas and I had left, so when it came to their wills, I fully intended to honour their final wishes.

Robert King was the man representing our aunts. He was a short, pudgy sort of man with a receding hairline. He might not have been much to look at but he was a damn good lawyer and had been representing our aunts for at least a decade, if not longer. Mr. King began the meeting by giving us his deepest sympathies for our loss.

"Please, how did they die, Mr. King? You didn't give us any details on the phone yesterday." I asked. Mr. King shifted in his seat as he contemplated how to begin.

"Yes, right, now, I was told everything by Ms. Miller, the young woman in your aunts' employment. If you have any more questions once we're done, she asked me to relay that she's more than happy to go over everything with the two of you." Mr. King paused to take a breath before continuing, "Betty had fallen ill with bronchitis a couple months ago, and unfortunately it turned into pneumonia. But, Betty being Betty refused to go to the hospital, even after it turned into pneumonia, so Ronnie was doing her best to care for her at home. Ahh... then the other day Betty took a turn for the worse and finally agreed to go to the emergency room for help. Ronnie called Ms. Miller around midnight to take them to the hospital. With Ms. Miller driving, and Ronnie and Betty in the back seat — they were only a few blocks from the hospital when another driver, heading out of the downtown area and not paying attention, ran a red light. He hit the passenger side of the car. Ronnie and Betty died from injuries sustained in the accident." Mr. King paused, settling his shaky voice. He had more to share but could see our hearts break with each word he uttered.

"Stubborn old bird," Thomas muttered as he stood from the table and paced over to the window running his hands through his hair to calm down. "If she had just gone to the hospital earlier," he said.

"Thomas, this... this is no one's fault. You know Betty... she hated doctors and hospitals. Of course she put it off for as long as possible." I tried to reason, with Thomas as well as myself. I wanted to reassure him, but scarcely believed the chain of events myself. He was right; Betty was too stubborn for her own good sometimes. I nodded to Mr. King to continue.

"Betty... Betty died on impact; and Ronnie... well Ronnie was pinned under the car and while the first responders managed to get her out and rushed to the hospital, she suffered significant injuries. I'm afraid the doctors did everything they could but she died during surgery."

Mr. King took a breath, having gotten the worst out and done with, allowing Thomas and I to absorb the details of what happened. Thomas was staring out the large window of the conference room, watching it rain while I sat in disbelief, desperately trying to make heads or tails of it all. I looked back to Mr. King, grief flooding my senses while questions began to fill my mind. I gave myself a moment to compose myself before responding to Mr. King.

"What... ahh... what happened... what happened to Ms. Miller and the other driver? The one who hit them... What happened to them?" My voice was shaky but I didn't care; I wanted to cry, to drink, to sleep. I wasn't quite sure which, but I needed to hear the rest. As I spoke, Thomas finally came back to the table, his eyes red from holding back tears while he listened to Mr. King's response.

"Well, the driver died at the scene. He sustained a fatal head injury, and..."

"Good. The bastard murdered our aunts, he deserved to die." Thomas spat out in anger, cutting Mr. King off mid-sentence.

"Thomas, come on. I know you are mad and I am too but still, it was an accident." I placed a hand on Thomas' shoulder in an attempt to calm him. Perhaps I should have let him be, but Thomas was never great at containing his temper and I did not want Mr. King to get the brunt of it. I knew Thomas needed to vent and Lord knew I needed to as well but it could all wait, it would all wait.

"And Ms. Miller?" I asked, trying to get us all back on track.

"Ms. Miller… she, she was the lucky one actually. She suffered a rather nasty concussion but other than that, just superficial cuts and bruises really. The doctors kept her for observation of the concussion but she's going to be just fine." Mr. King gave a small smile of comfort for the one sliver of good news out of the whole ordeal.

"That… that's good… ahh, good, I'm glad she's ok after… after everything," I muttered after a few silent seconds. Thomas was still shaking his head from the sequence of events. I found, for myself at least a small amount of comfort knowing that someone made it out okay.

"That's good? Really, Betty and Ronnie are dead! They are dead and you say that's good?" Thomas hollered at me, "Who cares if the girl working for them is fine? They're not!" I could see his temper rise.

"Yes Thomas, it's good that Ms. Miller is okay. She went through an ordeal. She was trying to help our aunts and didn't deserve this any more than they did. So yeah it's good!" I bawled back at him. Usually I was not one to raise my voice but we were both having a bad morning. Really, we were both having a bad week, but at this point, it couldn't be helped.

"Now, can we please finish going through their wills and be done here? Can we please just do that much?" I asked Thomas, hoping he'd sit back down so Mr. King could finish and we could all move on from this. It took Thomas a few dragged out seconds before he crossed his arms and finally sat back down. Mr. King looked at the two of us once more and started reading Betty and Ronnie's wills. Both were nearly identical. As expected, Thomas and I were to split most of their financial assets and properties fifty-fifty, but there were additional requests of me. In Betty's will, there was a three-fold request: First, I was to take over the operation of their bookshop in Victoria, British Columbia. Second, allow Miss Catherine Miller to continue to work there. And third, that Ms. Miller be given the sum of $20,000. Mr. King stated that this was in Betty's will because the shop was legally in her name and not Ronnie's, but the request came from both of them. When Mr. King read out this section, Thomas interjected.

"Why are our aunts giving $20,000 to a complete stranger? What right does she have to anything from Betty and Ronnie? And why... why is Michael singled out and left the bookshop?" I stared at my brother, dumbfounded and shocked. Complaining over a measly $20,000 and a bookshop he never cared for. A bookshop neither of us even needed. Mr. King addressed Thomas before I had a chance to say anything.

"Mr. Murphy, it is my understanding that Ms. Miller is the young woman who has been in their employment for nearly two years. Your aunts grew very fond of Ms. Miller and they were adamant in their wishes regarding her job at the bookstore and the $20,000." Mr. King paused to let Thomas take in the news for a second time.

"What does it even matter? This is what they wanted," I questioned.

"It matters, we don't even know this girl. Why would they want to give her money? Besides, she was driving — she's just as liable as that idiot who hit them. She should be arrested, not rewarded with twenty grand."

"Do you hear yourself? Ms. Miller was trying to help Ronnie and Betty and she was injured in that accident. She's far from liable. Besides this is what the aunts wanted so dammit I'm going to oblige."

"Mich—" Thomas began.

"Seriously. Get over it." I was done with this conversation. He was getting on my nerves but it could have just been me, my mind was on overload and I just wanted the day to be done already. "We will, of course, honour our aunt's wishes concerning Ms. Miller, Mr. King. Don't worry." My tone was firm and definitive, there was no room for Thomas to object.

Thomas was quick to show his disapproval, but I didn't care. I had no objections to Aunt Betty and Ronnie's request. If this was what they wanted then this was what was going to happen, no matter what. Though Thomas seemed to be having a hard time coming to terms with everything that was happening, this was not about him.

Thomas and I had entered that meeting with the same expectations but only one of us left disappointed with the outcome. For the rest of the day, I had to endure my brother's bad mood. He started to behave like a six-year-old who just had his favourite toy taken away. I knew there were things that needed to be done, arrangements for the funeral, which was taking place in Victoria where Betty and Ronnie had spent the last four years. That was the longest time they had spent anywhere. Thomas and I would have to go through their belongings, box up their lives, decide what to keep, and what to give away. I had to decide what to do with the bookshop. The idea of simply giving it to Ms. Miller crossed my mind, but if our aunts had wanted that surely they would have put that in the will. With the company growing and Hamish wanting to start expanding, I wasn't sure I had the time for a bookshop too, especially one in another country. But it was left to me, so I had to figure out something. Though it had been years, the thought of working in a bookshop again did sound nostalgically pleasing, and it couldn't possibly be more difficult then starting M&M Tech.

A small comfort had come to me when I learned that our aunts had pre-planned their funeral. All that was left for Thomas and I to do was show up. Mr. King had given me the address of the bookshop that also happened to be where Aunt Betty and Aunt Ronnie lived. As it turned out, the building they had bought with the store had an apartment upstairs. Mr. King also provided the address for the church and the pastor's contact information for the funeral.

I emailed him to set up a meeting for when Thomas and I got into town.

I was extremely curious about Ms. Miller, what kind of young woman was she to aid her employers in the middle of the night? That says a lot about a person; at least it did to me. Betty and Ronnie were obviously fond of her, how would she take the news about the money she had been left in their will, especially after what had happened?

That night, Thomas and I were packed and ready for our twelve-hour flight the following day. I gave Hamish a call, filling him in on the last couple of days and told him I was heading out of town for a few weeks. Hamish, of course, had no issue with me taking off and told me to let him know if there was anything he could do.

With nothing else to do before leaving, I went in search of a box I had been keeping in Thomas' storage area with the rest of my belongings. I found the box and headed back to the living room, putting it down on the coffee table. Thomas had already retired for the night, so I poured myself a glass of Pinot Noir, sat down, and opened the box. There were some old trinkets inside, papers I hadn't looked at in years, and a small old wooden chest with a broken metal lock. I pulled out the small wooden chest, removed the lock, and slowly opened the lid to examine what was inside.

Aunt Betty and I had always been rather close. Whenever she and Aunt Ronnie were away she would write, letting me know where they were and how they were doing. Betty and I began this tradition when I went off to college and was out on my own for the first time. That's why I was shocked to hear from Mr. King that Betty had been so ill, Betty and I kept up a regular correspondence. I had hoped we had the type of relationship where she would have told me something like that. There was a time when we discussed almost everything, but there were things I never confided to her. I never did tell her the whole story behind Robin and me getting divorced. Betty loved Robin, so I told her the divorce was no one's fault, we just grew apart and that it was all for the best. Aunt Betty wrote about how disappointed she was in me for letting the marriage dissolve, but she seemed to understand.

The wooden chest was full of her letters, I had kept them all over the years. Once a month I received a letter from her, letting me know how things were going, even when nothing had changed. When Mr. King read out the section of the will regarding Ms. Miller, her name resonated in my mind. I remembered Aunt Betty writing about her once. Digging through the pile of letters I finally found the one I remembered.

My dearest Michael,

I was sorry to hear about you and Robin. Is there really no way of repairing your marriage? You are not divorced yet, you haven't even started the proceedings, and you two could keep trying. After all, marriage is a sacred bond between two people, and such a bond should be honoured despite all of life's challenges. But then, I'm just an old woman with outdated beliefs, so what do I know. If Robin isn't the key to your happiness my boy, then I just hope one day you find it. Nothing is more important in life than being happy.

Speaking of happiness, my dear sister and I have finally found someone to help us out here in the shop (which is doing quite well, I might add). She's a lovely young woman who recently moved to the island. Her name is Catherine and she is just a darling. Now that she's here, Ronnie and I have no idea how we ever managed to get along without her. She's kind, hardworking and she certainly knows her books. At any rate, we have both readily fallen in love with her. Personally, had I ever been blessed with a daughter, I would have liked her to be like Catherine. I'm sure if you ever decide to come and visit your dear old aunts and meet her for yourself, you'll feel the same as we do. Anyway, we certainly think of her as our own. The poor thing has no family here and always seems so anxious; we have never met a young person as demure as Catherine. Regardless, she really is the sweetest thing.

Well my love, just a short letter this time. Ronnie and I continue to hope dear Thomas will stop being so adventuresome and settle down one of these days. Anyway, we are happy here in our little shop, and both of us are well, so you are not to worry as I know you do. Give Thomas our love. Do write soon, love hearing from you.

You're loving aunt,
Betty

I put the letter down and drank some of my wine. Of course Aunt Betty had written of Ms. Miller on other occasions but none of those letters elaborated details about her. Perhaps they never did learn much more about the young woman they had taken in.

I read the letter again along with some of the others from Aunt Betty trying to piece together a timeline, attempting to find some small clue she might have left. Berating myself for not staying in better contact, I wondered if she had attempted to tell me something more. Was I too caught up in my own life to see the signs? As sad and heartbroken as I was over their deaths, I found myself angry that Betty had not told me about her poor health, for not giving me the chance to help, and spend time with both her and Ronnie. And at the very least, the time to say goodbye.

CHAPTER TWO

Betty & Veronica's Books

THE TWELVE-HOUR FLIGHT from London to Victoria was long and tedious; we had a layover in Toronto. I found the flight to be smooth enough. I always loved flying, being so high in the air, believing the world could not affect me from thirty-four thousand feet above it all. Thomas on the other hand, well Thomas doesn't travel well. He finds the planes too confining, even though we tend to fly first-class. After taking off from Heathrow he complained and continued to fume and pout about our argument yesterday. I imagined smacking him a time or two and telling him to get over it as he prattled on the entire flight. I suppose it was my inner child stirring from our loss.

Besides Thomas, the flight was fine. We arrived on time and quickly got a cab to take us to Betty and Ronnie's place, which was about thirty minutes from us, right downtown. The cab dropped us off in front of an old brick building at the end of Johnson Street. Thomas and I stared up at the aged building and read the wooden sign hanging just over the door:

Betty & Veronica's Books

Standing in front of the old brick building, looking up at it, I understood why Betty and Ronnie had been attracted to it. Like them, the building was old-fashioned and held a deep beauty after generations of standing. In that brief moment, I was proud and happy to have been left such a building and was very glad my aunts had chosen it.

For the first time all week, Thomas and I wanted the same thing, sleep. Between the woes of the week and the jet lag, we were both done-in. The door to the shop was open and as we entered, I couldn't help but breathe in all the books. That old leather scent filled the air and I felt like I was home, just how it used to be when I was a boy.

The store gave the illusion of being small and cramped. From floor to ceiling there were books; old, new, and used. From the classics to new-age, and the very rare to everyday books, their collection had certainly grown since I had last seen Betty and Veronica. A soft, warm light filled the shop. Right at the entrance there was a small counter holding an old vintage cash register with books stacked on either side. A couple of feet behind the counter was a wooden staircase that presumably led to the second and third floors of the building. The shop itself was deep. Looking down the thin hallway of stacks, I felt as though it went on forever.

We dropped our luggage by the door and took in our new surroundings — that's when we saw her — Catherine Miller. She gradually came down the wooden staircase reading a book. I know how that sounds, of course, but it is precisely how it was. Ms. Miller was beautiful, with long, chocolate brown, wavy hair, and a soft fair complexion with dark, hazel eyes. She wore a light blue dress that stopped just above her knees, with a thin black belt around her waist to accent her hourglass figure and a pair of simple black heels on her feet. So engrossed by the book in her hand, she was a vision. I was reminded of the story, *Beauty and the Beast* and couldn't help but see a resemblance between Ms. Miller and Belle. She made her way down the stairs.

"Oh! Hello, sorry about that, didn't hear you two come in." She set her book down on the counter as she spoke. "Welcome to Betty and Veronica's Books. How may I help you?" Her voice was soft, like her smile, which revealed a small dimple on her right cheek. Looking at her closely, I could see the bruises from the car accident, but her make-up did a good job covering most of them. To my dismay, Thomas spoke first:

"Are you, Catherine Miller? We're Betty and Ronnie's nephews."

I watched Thomas' demeanour change as he spoke to Ms. Miller, flashing his eye-catching smile. I couldn't believe it. Thomas had done nothing but complain about Ms. Miller for the last two days and as soon as he saw her decided she was his next conquest. I was exhausted, with my mind so crowded from recent events, and the utter lack of sleep the last few days, this was more than I could take. But I also had a feeling he was up to something. Turning into Casanova, regardless of the fact that Ms. Miller wasn't even his type, though she was a beautiful woman. Thomas had always gravitated towards those more attainable, dim-witted, more beauty than brains types. Ms. Miller didn't strike me as that kind of woman. No, if Thomas was wooing her, it meant he had something up his sleeve. At least she didn't seem to be falling for any of his charms.

"Right, yes of course." It seemed to me, she was caught off guard but quickly composed herself. "It's nice to finally meet you both, though perhaps under better circumstances. I'm very sorry for your loss. Betty and Ronnie were... well, they were wonderful women. They will be truly missed." It looked as though tears had begun to form in her eyes, but she held them back.

"Thank you" I managed to squeeze out before Thomas started talking again.

"Well, Ms. Miller, I know I speak for my brother as well as myself when I say just how grateful we are for all you've done for our dear aunts." Thomas sounded so sleazy and fake. It was appalling he could even think of acting this way. Our aunts had just passed, Catherine had been the one to look after them, and she was still clearly recovering from the accident herself. I was powerless to do more than stand there astounded at his complete lack of propriety. Luckily Catherine seemed utterly indifferent to his advances.

"Your aunts have been very good to me, we all became very close." She gave another soft smile that also seemed dismissive, but Thomas didn't seem to notice. Watching Catherine, I got the sense she was quite used to men hitting on her. Ms. Miller composed herself well in the awkward situation Thomas was certainly creating. I had the impression she'd had quite enough of my brother.

"Ah, Ms. Miller, would you mind showing us up to our aunts flat by chance?" I kept my tone as light and friendly as possible, trying to make up for Thomas who was shooting me foul looks for interrupting whatever he was babbling on about.

"Of course, please follow me." Catherine said as she headed towards the stairs. Thomas and I grabbed our bags to follow.

When we reached the top of the landing we saw more rows of books, another floor of the shop. The shelves of books nearly reached the ceiling. This section of the hall seemed to be action and adventure on one side with a horror mystery section on the other. The first door on the right at the top of the stairs led to the historical, fiction and biographies. We followed Catherine down the hallway, passing two open doors that revealed more and more books.

When we reached the end of the corridor, Catherine took us up a second stairwell to our left leading to an open landing that presented a loft-style apartment. The kitchen, dining, and living areas were open, flowing into one. There were doors for two bedrooms and a bath, a number of large windows, and a couple of skylights that filled the living area with light. The atmosphere was open and fresh. The old-fashioned furniture really suited the traditional architecture of the building. Everything reflected Betty and Ronnie — classic and loved.

Thomas and I put our bags down and Catherine said, "I'll let you both rest... umm, if you need anything I'll just be downstairs." She left with another soft smile. Once she was gone I turned to Thomas, curious as to what he thought he was playing at.

"What's the matter with you? What was all that about down there?"

Thomas smirked, "I'm just getting to know the young thing. After all, our aunts were rather generous to her."

"My God! Is that all it was about? You thought you could seduce her out of the will, did you? Come on! She's nice, so nice that she's been taking care of our aunts while you've been shagging half of London. So please Thomas, none of your games, just leave her be."

"Hey, she's cute. You never know, perhaps I fancy her?"

"Fancy her? Seriously, you don't even know her. For Christ's sake, Thomas, you hated the mere idea of her just two days ago. Besides, she's not even your type. Just leave it be."

"Not... not my type! Damn Michael, she's a beautiful woman, I'd say that pretty much sums up my type right there."

"Oh come off it, when have you ever gone for the quiet bookworm? And, I hardly need to mention that the girl can't be more than twenty-eight or twenty-nine years-old. You're forty-five. Do you really think she'll go for you?"

"First of all, I do go for simple bookish women."

"Since when? I can't even remember the last time you dated a woman who read more than a fashion magazine."

"Magazines count."

"Thomas..."

"And second, all women go for older and sophisticated men, especially ones like me."

"Older definitely, but sophisticated? I'll hold judgment on that one. But come on, please don't do whatever it is your thinking of doing."

"Oh, what do you care anyway?"

"Thomas, I do not... I will not see that girl hurt just because you have a petty grudge. She took care of Betty and Ronnie in case you've forgotten, and she deserves better than your shenanigans. Now, we're here to say goodbye to our aunts, deal with all their belongings and give that girl what is rightfully hers. So, no ploys, no plans, no schemes! Just leave her well alone."

"It's a matter of principle. That girl is not family. She has no right to the money. For all we know she swindled her way into that will."

"Do you hear yourself? Really? You're being ridiculous. God, you sound just like father, talking about family money and all that. Do you realize that? You can't honestly believe that Catherine did anything but care for Betty and Ronnie. Besides, what's your grand plan anyway? Get close to her while we're here and convince her not to take what's rightfully hers?"

"Maybe..."

"Fine, fine you know what, do what you like because I bet she won't even look twice at you. She's not going to fall for any of your tricks. No, something tells me you are not her type in any way, shape or form."

"Not her type! Please, I'm every woman's type, handsome, rich, worldly. No woman can resist a chance with me. But okay, if you think I can't get her, I'll take that bet."

"Bet? What bet?"

"$20,000. The sum our aunts left Ms. Catherine. If I can win her, have her fall for me and convince her not to take that money, then I get the twenty-thousand."

Thomas' smugness was oozing out of him. He was so convinced that he could win. I, on the other hand, had absolutely no faith in his plan. I don't know why I did it. Betting on a woman, whatever the reason it never ends well and this was no exception. Now I should have known better, I should have just let it be and left Thomas to his idiotic scheme. But I didn't. Instead, I did this:

"And if you can't?"

"Not possible."

"Say it is."

"Fine, in that extremely unlikely situation, I will give you the $20,000."

"In addition to the twenty we will be giving Ms. Miller?"

"What? No."

"Thomas?"

"Fine, fine. In addition to," Thomas said through gritted teeth.

See, stupid move on my part. I should have just left it all well enough alone, but at that moment, the thought of Thomas losing $40,000 was just too good to pass up. Now, I regretted the bet the moment we made it. It was trashy and demeaning towards Catherine, but it was too late.

"Oh, and you're forgetting one other thing we have to do while we're here."

"Yeah, what's that?" I was irritable and drained at this point. With no sleep and jet-lagged, I was beyond done with my brother.

"Well, we have to decide how much to sell this place for. Given the location, I think we can get a good price and make a little extra off this place?" Thomas gestured to our surroundings as he spoke.

"Sell? I am not selling. Do you hear me? Not. Selling. What makes you think you have any say with what I do with the shop and loft? In case you've forgotten, this place was left to me, not you. If you recall, Betty and Ronnie didn't want the place sold. They wanted me to keep the place and let Ms. Miller stay on for as long as she wanted. So tell me, how the hell can she keep working here if I sell it?" I was almost yelling at Thomas as I spoke. His presumptuous arrogance thinking he should be included in my decisions pushed me over the edge, and I completely lost my temper. Grabbing the first object I could, regrettably a book, and threw it at him. Thomas ducked, laughing at my attempt.

"Oh come on, what are you going to do with a bookshop? I know, we could sell to Miss whatever for the low, low sum of $20,000. How's that for an idea? If you're not interested in making a profit that is."

"You're despicable, you know that. Look I don't know what I'm going to do yet, but whatever it is you can be damn sure it will be the right thing."

"The right thing? What's that supposed to mean?"

"Pretty much the complete opposite of whatever you would do."

I threw my hands in the air and walked away from him at that point, tired of arguing. We simply couldn't see eye to eye on anything these days. Well, truth be told, Thomas and I hadn't seen eye to eye on anything since we started my divorce proceedings.

I knew that Thomas would do his damnedest to win our bloody bet regarding Ms. Miller. Deep down I knew it would end badly, but what is done is done. It didn't really surprise me, Thomas' machinations. He always did what he pleased without any consideration of others, not caring who he might hurt in the process. He would get exactly what he wanted and clearly had no intention of honouring our aunt's final wishes. No, he wanted me to sell the shop and oust Ms. Miller. I had to admit, I was finding it harder and harder to recognize my own brother. I walked away, in search of Betty's room, leaving Thomas to his own callousness. Much like the rest of the building, Aunt Betty and Aunt Ronnie's loft was full of books. Not nearly as many as in the shop, but here the books were their personal collection.

Although I had never been in this particular room, it was clearly Betty's. Always the same décor as every home she had lived in. The room had a four-poster bed directly under the window with a small table on either side. There was a solid armoire on the far right wall and a small vanity on the left, with all of her perfumes and makeup sitting on top. The side tables both held a lamp. The left side table was stacked with books. Her favourite, Jane Eyre was sitting right on top. I hid away in Aunt Betty's room for an hour or so, slowly going through some of her books, remembering my youthful days spent with Betty and Ronnie. I knew I couldn't stay there forever. I would have to venture out at some point and face Thomas again. We had a lot to do, but first, we had to tell Ms. Miller about the will and there was no way I was going to let Thomas do that.

I emerged from Betty's room to find Thomas asleep on the couch. I thought of waking him but then thought better of it. We'd only argue again, and it would be easier to speak to Ms. Miller without him. There was much to discuss and Thomas would only be a hindrance. So I moved past him, quietly so as not to wake him, and headed downstairs.

When I came down the stairs, I expected to see Ms. Miller sitting behind the counter reading her book, but she wasn't. I slowly moved around the overflowing, quaint little bookshop in search of her. I ventured down the thin hallway until I reached another room. This backroom was slightly easier to maneuver. It was large, with columns of stacks filled with books against every wall and lined up in aisles. I slowly made my way through each aisle until I found Catherine. She was kneeling on the floor, books lying all around her while she held one in her hands, lost deep within the pages. I assumed she had been reorganizing the bottom shelf before getting distracted, as it was half-empty in front of her. She was utterly absorbed in the book. As her eyes moved across each page, her lips silently formed each word she came across. I gently cleared my throat making my presence known to her. I said, "Hello" startling her. I immediately apologized.

"No," she said after a second, "It's alright. I should have been paying attention anyway."

"Got caught up, did you?" I asked, referencing the book in her hands.

"Yes," she smiled, "it looks like a second edition, couldn't resist, *Northanger Abbey*, my favourite," she said indicating the book.

I knelt down next to Catherine and noticed how she shifted slightly away as I did so. As there was plenty of room I figured she must just like her personal space.

"I love that one too," I told her. "It's my favourite Austen actually. Betty used to read it to me when I was a kid." Catherine offered the book for me to examine; and she was right, it looked to be at least a second edition.

"You must miss them?" Catherine asked softly.

"I do," I said and handed her back *Northanger Abbey* careful not to lose her page.

"Well for what it's worth, I really am sorry. They were wonderful."

"Thank you. You must miss them too. I understand you became very close to them?"

"Yes... yes, I miss them. Your aunts were very good to me. They took me in and treated me like family. They will never fully know how much I needed that, needed them." I wanted to ask her more, but before I could, she changed the subject.

"Are you all rested from your flight?"

"Not yet, but I'd rather sleep tonight and try to bypass the jet lag. Thomas is sleeping. He doesn't travel well." Catherine nodded in understanding as I continued.

"Um, there is something you need to know Ms. Miller —" She cut me off to say,

"Catherine, please Mr. Murphy."

"Alright, Catherine. And please, it's Michael. There's no need for all that Mr. Murphy stuff, well perhaps with my brother." She smiled as we both gave a slight chuckle at the statement.

"Yes, your brother is... well forgive me for saying so, but he seems to be rather full of himself or fond of himself... maybe both, I can't quite tell." Catherine chuckled quietly as we shared another small laugh.

"Yes, I'm very sorry for his display earlier. Being his brother isn't easy... he's pretty much a narcissist, always needing to be the centre of attention. Though he comes off as quite the self-important dolt, it does make him an amazing lawyer."

"Yes, that's right. Thomas is the lawyer, also the eldest. You have your own computer company and are married. Your aunts talked a great deal about both of you."

"I bet they did... except I'm not married anymore, or at least I won't be once the divorce papers go through. She and I signed just before Thomas and I got the news about Betty and Ronnie." I felt like I was oversharing but there was no way to backtrack.

"Oh, I'm sorry. I..."

"Nothing to be sorry for... really, I'm better off. There is something I do want to talk about though. Just before Thomas and I left London, we sat down with Mr. King, Betty and Ronnie's lawyer, and while going through their wills a couple of things came up."

"The bookstore..."

"Yes the shop. The shop has been left to me actually. Betty and Ronnie requested that I take over and honour their wish for you to be kept on. I want you to know that you have a place here for as long as you like."

"That's very kind."

"Well, there is actually one other thing concerning you and the will. Betty and Ronnie left you $20,000."

Catherine sat quietly in disbelief. I sat with her in silence while she processed the new information. After a moment, she responded.

"That's... ah... that's surprising"

"Yes, it was to us as well. But it's clear just how much Betty and Ronnie valued you."

"I see." Catherine's tone took an unexpected edge, surprising me.

She quickly finished putting the books back on the shelf, standing upright while still holding onto *Northanger Abbey*. I stood up alongside her, careful to give her space as she moved past me. I followed her down the hallway trying to wrap my head around what just happened. Everything was going fine and then she seemed to shut down. I replayed the conversation in my mind to see if I had insulted her unintentionally somewhere along the way, but if I did, I couldn't figure out where.

"Well...." I started as we travelled down the thin hallway, "They loved you. I know Betty spoke very fondly of you. They both thought of you quite as their own and they clearly wanted to make sure you were taken care of." I couldn't help but feel the more I spoke the more closed off and upset she became.

"Taken care of, clearly," Catherine said, her voice cracking and her rigid tone filled the room around us. She was not taking any of this the way I had expected.

"No, I didn't mean taken care of in a... but they didn't want... ugh... I just mean..."

"Oh no, of course not. Look, I don't work here for the salary. And I did not make friends with your aunts, and care for them all this time just for a potential payday." She sounded hurt and was getting defensive as she spoke.

"No, I wasn't suggesting..."

"Look, I cared very much for Betty and Ronnie. They were the closest thing I came to having a real family."

We had come back to the main room and I could see tears beginning to form in her eyes. I was confused as to how our pleasant conversation had taken such a turn. Why had Catherine taken such offence to my aunts' generosity?

"Catherine, I have absolutely no doubt that you had a great deal of love and affection for Betty and Ronnie. And please, I never meant 'to imply that you had any ill-conceived motive toward them." I gently touched her arm in an attempt to display my sincerity and try to re-establish the connection we seemed to have lost. Catherine backed away instantly, anxiety and panic flooding her delicate features.

"I'm... I'm sorry... I'm..." Mid-sentence, Catherine interrupted my apology.

"No, I'm sorry, I'm... I don't um... I don't like being touched... I... people don't touch me." She fell silent, and I could have sworn, for a split second there was a hint of shame in her eyes before her features became vacant. Catherine Miller baffled me. With every look I caught from her, I grew more and more curious about the enigma that was this interesting and complex young woman.

"Please I'm sorry. It will not happen again, I promise." I raised my hands slightly in front of me before purposely placing them behind my back and taking a step back in a show of good faith. I had never met someone quite as guarded, as she seemed to be. I was only just beginning to see just how tentative and cautious she was. Catherine relaxed a bit after my gesture. I could not help but wonder what might have happened to her to create such a reserved demeanour.

"I'm gonna take a break, grab some coffee." Catherine headed towards the front door and walked out, still clutching the copy of *Northanger Abbey*.

"Very smooth Michael." I turned around to see Thomas standing in the middle of the staircase. "You never were all that great with the ladies were you?" He gave a sharp laugh. "Trying to get in there before I take a shot I see? Because you know I will win in the end — you don't stand a chance." Thomas said smugly.

"You really are a shallow bastard, you know that right? I'm not trying to win her. I was simply telling her about the will."

"She took it well from what I saw."

"Not as expected, no. She's complex."

"Complex?"

"Yes, Thomas, complex. You won't be able to sweep her off her feet as you do most women. She's... she's... I'm not sure. She's something."

"Well she's still a woman, and there I have never failed. Mark my words Michael — I will win — I always win."

Thomas smiled at me knowingly then wandered back upstairs, leaving me alone in the quiet, empty shop.

CHAPTER THREE

Funerals

CATHERINE MOSTLY KEPT to herself in the following few days. Thomas made more embarrassing attempts to charm her, with little success. She showed no interest in any of his propositions. Nor did she show much interest in me for that matter. I had decided to just let things lie since our last regrettable encounter. Thomas continued to insist I should have left everything to him as he could have achieved a better outcome, but I stood by my decision. Thomas would have made a bigger mess of things then I had.

Since my conversation with Catherine, and observing her over the days we had been there, I knew I would have to build her trust and it would take an immense amount of time. She was very isolated from the world. She scarcely said two words to anyone, excluding the odd customer who came into the shop. I kept thinking of Betty and Ronnie, trying to figure out how they had made a connection with her. I tried to see her the way my aunts would have and began to understand. Catherine was quiet, very quiet; you could miss her in a room if you didn't know to look for her. Betty and Ronnie would have loved that. When Thomas and I were younger helping out in the bookshop, they would always tell us we were too loud. I learned to be quiet but Thomas never did, he was far too boisterous.

The day before the funeral Thomas and I had our meeting with Pastor William Sharp over at the church. The meeting didn't take long, it was just for us to all sit down and make sure everything was in order. Betty and Ronnie had pre-arranged their funerals so Pastor Sharp simply walked us through everything they had planned. We did not intend to make any changes. The funeral was to be a small ceremony, with Thomas, myself and a few friends celebrating their lives, sharing stories of the two lovely old women who owned the bookstore. Betty and Ronnie had already been cremated so their ashes were to sit at the front of the room, in beautiful urns they had picked themselves, on view for everyone to see. Pastor Sharp wanted to know which one of us was going to give the eulogy. To be honest, neither Thomas nor I had even thought of it. In the end, it was agreed that Thomas would give the eulogy because according to him, "I'm a successful lawyer and comfortable with public speaking. Michael here would only screw it up."

After the eulogy, others would have the opportunity to share their favourite memories and tales of our aunts. Then everyone would move to a different section of the church for coffee, tea, and finger foods to reminisce over Betty and Ronnie. Frankly, I just hoped everything would simply go as planned.

By the time Thomas and I were back from the church, I found a note from Catherine taped to the front door. I took a brief moment to read it and admire her beautiful delicate handwriting before handing it to Thomas.

Mr. T. Murphy & Mr. M. Murphy,

Sorry for not being here when you get back. The store was dead so I closed up a half-hour early. Everything is clean and fully stocked. The till has been cashed out and locked up in the safe.

Ms. Miller

"Who does she think she is closing up early and just leaving like that?" Thomas spat out.

"It's half-past four, she only closed up thirty minutes early. It's fine."

"Why would she bother to close up early anyway? I mean really, from what I gather this shop is the only thing in that girl's life."

"Thomas!"

"No, you know I'm right, you're too soft when it comes to people. Come on, tell me I'm wrong. Name one thing you've learned about that girl that doesn't involve this shop?"

I paused for a moment, desperately trying to think of something to prove Thomas wrong. Regrettably, I couldn't think of anything.

"She's just private is all, nothing wrong with that and I am not soft."

"Oh yes you are, one look at that girl and you lost all backbone."

"Oh please, like you care anyway."

I left Thomas down in the shop and headed upstairs to continue sorting through the loft.

The funeral was the next day. With the shop closed, Thomas and I had plenty of time to get ready. Betty and Ronnie's ashes were already at the church and the caterers were handling the rest. All we had to do was show up. Thomas and I put on our black suits and headed to church to say goodbye to the two women who had practically raised us.

The walk to the church didn't take long, it was only a few blocks away and when we got there we found the place was already full of people who had known and loved Betty and Ronnie. It took us awhile to make our way through the crowd as people kept stopping us to give their condolences. We hardly knew anyone. I recognized a few names from Aunt Betty's letters but for the most part, Thomas and I couldn't keep anyone straight. Once we were shown our seats, we headed back to the front doors to greet more people.

As we stood there talking to person after person, I couldn't help but notice that Catherine hadn't shown up yet. Though I shouldn't have been, I half worried she wouldn't come at all due to our current rocky state. While I continued to scan the room for Catherine's arrival, my eye caught sight of Hamish MacPhail of all people, stroll up the church steps and into the main area.

Hamish and I met in the first year and hit it off. How we became friends was a bit odd. I had been wandering the campus, lost in search of the library when I stumbled across a group of people all huddled in a circle. I decided to see what all the commotion was about and I saw this six-two broad shouldered, short carrot red hair and scruffy short-trimmed beard in jeans and a *ZZ Top* shirt mouthing off at two guys. I could only make out every second word Hamish was saying. I was still fairly new to Edinburgh and was struggling with all the thick accents around me, but Hamish's speech had always been gruffer than most others, and he likes to spur people with quick slang which didn't help anyone in understanding him. From what I understood, Hamish had been sleeping with the one guy's lass and got caught. As I watched the three guys, I could see a fight was about to break out. I would find out through the years that this was rather common for him. He is an annoyingly clever person with little to no filter, so tends to find himself in trouble from time to time, but now, I'm usually around to help get out of anything too serious. Then, I saw the fight coming and stepped in to try and help the guy out. We both got our asses handed to us, but Hamish and I ended up lifelong friends.

Attending the funeral, Hamish was wearing his family MacPhail kilt with its crisp reds and deep forest greens with tints of light blue and pale white weaved throughout the plaid pattern, paired with a simple white button shirt and black blazer. His tall stature and broad shoulders had nearly every woman in the church looking his way. He removed his black sunglasses revealing his deep electric blue eyes, soft and full of sorrow for the loss of two old women he cherished.

"Michael!" Hamish immediately hugged his friend. "I'm so sorry mucker, they really were terrific old birds." Hamish released me and shook Thomas' hand in condolence. "Thomas, I feel for ya."

"Hamish." Thomas shook his hand, nodding his head in thanks.

"I can't believe you came. What about Susan? I didn't think she'd let you out of her sight." We chuckled, both knowing how possessive Hamish's girlfriend was.

"Na, we broke up last week, was gonna tell ya but you've had a lot on lately. Susan, she was a touch too intense for me ya know, wantin' to know me every whereabouts and whatnot. It was too constraining, ya know? I gotta be free. Besides your aunts were stoakin' ladies. I had a lot ah respect for those two, great shame them goin' out an all. Couldn't miss this, nor let ya go through it all with just Thomas." Hamish caught the look flash across Thomas' face and realized he said too much again. "Och sorry mucker. But you're not exactly the best when it comes to emotional support an' aw."

"You just say the first thing that comes to your mind there don't you MacPhail?" Thomas shot at Hamish along with a nasty look before walking away from us to greet the others walking into the church.

"Touchy." Hamish smiled as he looked around the room.

"Hamish…" I was about to defend Thomas when I saw Catherine walking up the church steps, and she wasn't alone. Thomas was back at my side before I could even blink, having spotted Catherine himself.

"Awe, it's your wannabe girlfriend." Thomas sneered into my ear before Catherine entered the church. Hamish turned, curious to see who we were staring at.

Catherine came in and headed straight toward the three of us. I got the sense she was still wary around us and after all, I couldn't really blame her. Thomas and I had successfully made complete asses of ourselves in the span of one afternoon. She had every right to be cautious. Now, I know that I shouldn't have been admiring Catherine at my aunt's funeral but I couldn't help myself. Even grief-stricken, she was lovely. Her wavy hair was up in a loose clip and she wore a little black knee-length dress with a slim blue belt around her waist. Looking at her, I knew I wanted to redeem myself and it had nothing to do with the bet. I was drawn to her smile, her fondness for books and yes, her beauty. I also had the distinct feeling that she would never want me, the man who insulted her so quickly upon meeting her. Beyond that, Catherine didn't even seem interested in any romantic attachments, she kept to herself. No men ever came around to see her, and all of Thomas's attempts always ended in refusal. I decided my fascination with her was nothing more than an innocent crush that I needed to get over.

It wasn't until she was standing in front of us that I noticed the girl she had come in with. She seemed to be the complete opposite of Catherine. Here stood a tall sturdy woman with straight, long black hair and emerald green eyes. She wore black leggings with a short wavy black skirt that had silver sparkles all over, and a dark purple blouse that struggled to contain her robust chest. Her name was Zoey Johnson and she was Catherine's best friend and roommate. Zoey, unlike Catherine, was very talkative and seemed to speak her mind quite freely. Right away, you could tell Zoey was a bubbly person, who seemed to care deeply for those around her. She jumped in and introduced herself; explained how she was Catherine's best friend and worked in the cafe next door to the bookshop. As Zoey offered her condolences, I found my eyes drifting back to Catherine. Catherine was looking down at the floor while Zoey spoke vivaciously with Hamish. She only looked up at all of us when it was time to find our seats. Hamish tailed after Catherine and Zoey, sitting with them and chatting up Zoey the entire time. I could see it already, Hamish loved women, all women, and Zoey seemed to be a match for his own gregarious character.

Once it was time to begin, Thomas and I took our seats and watched as the service began. I have to admit it was great to see so many people there for Betty and Ronnie. Hearing their stories, I felt a sense of peace knowing that in their final years they were surrounded by friends who truly knew and loved them. In just a short period, they had become a part of this community. They had affected so many lives. I had never felt prouder to be their nephew. And then, Thomas stood up and gave the eulogy. Pleasantly surprised by his kind words towards our aunts, it felt like days since I'd seen him act even remotely respectfully. Perhaps, he'd finally drop his callous facade and show his true self, whatever, whoever that might be. Maybe our aunts' death would change him for the better.

Overall, the service wasn't too long and everything seemed to go smoothly. I found the reception seemed to drag on a bit. I was out of my comfort zone being stuck in a room full of strangers. For a good part of the time, I sat alone with a cup of tea watching Zoey guide Catherine around the room, speaking enthusiastically to everyone while keeping an eye out for Hamish. Zoey was trying to get Catherine to smile, telling tales of the two old women who had taken her in and become friends. I couldn't help but wonder: *how on earth had Zoey of all people manage to befriend Catherine? For that matter, how had Catherine decided Zoey was the friend for her?*

As the reception wound down and everyone started to head home for the evening, Thomas and Pastor Sharp came to me each holding an urn. As Pastor Sharp handed me Aunt Betty, I knew it was time to go. I searched for Hamish but he had disappeared, likely with Zoey. Thomas and I walked back to the shop in silence carrying our aunts' urns carefully. It wasn't until we were back up in the loft that Thomas broke our silence.

"So, figure out what to do with this old place yet?" Thomas asked as he poured himself a finger of scotch from the bar cabinet.

"Thomas." I retorted.

"Oh come on, you need to make a decision before we go home," he said in between sips of scotch.

"Yes, but not today. I mean, we just came back from our aunts' funeral. Can we not just have this one day?"

"Hey, I loved Betty and Ronnie, you know I did. They gave us the best life we could have asked for. We saw the world, thanks to those two. But life moves on. We are still living and this place is a potential goldmine if we sell it to the right buyer… a developer, maybe? I mean its prime real estate."

"No, and no. I'm not going to sell the shop just so it can get turned into condos. Can we just discuss this tomorrow, please? Today I want to remember Betty and Ronnie and have a toast in their names."

"Michael, come on, when was the last time we even saw them? It's been years."

"You haven't seen them in years but I kept in touch with them. Remember they both came out to visit us just last year — oh wait, you were too busy for the get-together. And just because you choose to ignore your emotions does not mean the rest of the world does." Thomas stared at me for a long moment, then he started to laugh.

"Oh, oh I get it. It's that girl, isn't it? You like her but you know you don't have a hope in hell with her, so you're keeping this place just be near her and hope that one day she'll notice you." Thomas continued laughing. I tried to rebuke his accusation no matter how true his words were. Thomas had a knack for getting under my skin, always knew just what buttons to push. I placed the ashes of Aunt Betty down on the table before turning back to Thomas.

"This has absolutely nothing to do with Ms. Miller and everything to do with the fact that you seem to have no regard for the feelings of others. If our aunts had wanted the place sold, they would have said so. And quite frankly, since you brought up Ms. Miller, I'm calling off our bet. I am not going to let you attempt to take away what is rightfully hers, and I will not risk you hurting her, she has clearly been through a lot." I was fuming. My anger and grief beyond control, but directed at Thomas.

"Just because you don't think you can win our little bet does not mean you can just call it off, Michael."

"You're not hearing me, Thomas. The bet is off and I believe it would be best if you went back to London."

"Ah, I see. How about I just go back to London and leave you here with that girl?"

"You know I really don't think that either of us has a chance with her and we should just leave her alone. So how about you remember that we just came from our aunt's funeral and leave it there for today."

"Come off it, you're just pissed because I can actually get women, unlike you. At least my women don't leave me for their divorce lawyer."

"That's low Thomas, even for you. For the record, the only reason the women in your life don't leave you, is because you don't ever stick around long enough to give them a chance. I'm done arguing with you. The bet is off and that is the end of it."

I walked around Thomas in a frenzy, grabbing the bottle of whiskey from the bar cabinet. I was about to head back to Aunt Betty's room to drink my bitter day away when we saw Catherine standing on the landing with a shocked look upon her face.

CHAPTER FOUR

Mystery Girl

I WOKE THE following morning hungover, if not still slightly drunk, and feeling like shit. Drowning myself in whiskey did nothing to help my sour mood. I got up slowly and went to stand in the shower for a good twenty minutes attempting to wake-up and get rid of my pounding headache. After my shower, I managed to pull on a pair of old faded jeans and a simple grey t-shirt for comfort's sake. It was as presentable as I could get that morning. I tried to mentally prepare for Thomas. I knew we'd have to finish our argument at some point. I just wasn't sure when I'd be ready for it.

Stepping into the morning lit living room and seeing Thomas sitting at the kitchen bar with a cup of coffee and the morning paper, put me right off. I was holding a grudge from the day before. I was still in a sour mood and not quite ready yet to talk, so I did the very brotherly, albeit childish thing, and ignored him. Thomas, in turn, took very little notice of me as I passed him heading out of the loft and down into the shop. It was too early for the shop to open or Catherine to be in so I made my way to the front door and headed out in search of coffee. I figured a strong cup of coffee was just what I needed to get through my day.

It was brighter than I had expected when I stepped outside. I chastised myself for not grabbing my sunglasses, but I was definitely not going back for them. I headed next door to the coffee shop and as I adjusted to the light, read the sign hanging above the door:

ZZZ Up Coffee
Open Early, Open Late

ZZZ Up Coffee was conveniently right next door and happened to make the best cup of coffee in the city. I walked into the quaint little coffee shop with brightly coloured walls of greens and purples, only to see Catherine, Zoey and Hamish sitting at one of the tables near the counter having a cup and engaged in conversation. They all looked up as I walked in due to the little bell that rang whenever someone entered or exited the cafe. Zoey greeted me with a bright smile, wishing a good morning as she headed behind the counter to get me a cup of coffee. Catherine, on the other hand, hardly took notice of me and finished her coffee. She stood from her chair acknowledging me for the first time in days.

"I should go and open up," she said and turned to Zoey. "Thanks for the coffee, hon. I'll see you later, Hamish." Catherine smiled at Hamish before she grabbed her purse off the back of her chair and left. I turned to watch her leave, forgetting where I was and what Zoey had said during my daze.

"Sorry," I said, hoping she'd repeat herself.

"I said she doesn't trust you, yet. Don't worry she'll get there, you just have to give her time... Coffee?" Zoey was clearly a morning person.

"Please" I replied, "she... she ah, told you then?"

"Oh yeah, but I wouldn't worry about it, took me over a year to get her to trust me and we were roommates. So you just have to go at her pace. It will be fine." Zoey handed me a coffee.

"Sorry," I said again.

"Look, you have to understand Catherine adored your aunts. From what I can tell, she didn't have much before meeting them. Betty and Ronnie helped Catherine get back on her feet. They brought her over to my place asking if she could stay with me. I had an empty room so I figured why not. She was super quiet, super shy and it took me months to get her to even make small talk with me. Now we are best friends. My point is, Catherine takes time to warm to people, so don't fret too much about it, okay? Just apologize, give it some time and she'll come around."

I set myself down next to Hamish feeling like a complete muppet.

"So you don't really know anything about her then? Her past? Nothing prior to her coming here?" I asked.

"It doesn't matter what I know, I wouldn't tell you, that's for her to decide who she wants to let in. And if she wants to keep her past to herself who am I to pry. I know who she is in the here and now, and she's amazing. So I'm not going to meddle for curiosity's sake. What kind of friend would I be if I bullied her into talking about things she'd clearly rather not? I let her come to me with things when she's ready, and I suggest, Mr. Murphy, that you and your brother do the same."

"Understood Miss Johnson." I gave Zoey a knowing smile, appreciating all the advice given and consciously decided to heed her warning and keep my personal questions about Catherine to myself. Zoey went back behind the counter to get ready for the morning rush she knew was coming.

"Nothing to add there, Hamish? You stayed uncharacteristically quiet throughout all that?" I questioned Hamish, knowing he was never one to keep his mouth shut.

"Oh no, not on this one, never argue with a hen." Hamish winked over at Zoey while she wiped the countertop down.

"I take it she's the reason I lost track of you after the funeral yesterday?"

"Yeah, sorry we got to talkin' and just hit it off. I just... she's a bampot and I mean in all the right ways. I really think she's the one, mucker."

"The one? Like Susan was the one? Hamish, you met her yesterday, you two haven't even known each other for twenty-four hours yet."

"Nah, Zoey is so much cooler than Susan, plus she doesn't seem to have that stalker-y boil-your-bunny feel to her, unlike Susan. Man was I wrong 'bout that lass. But not Zoey, I'm tellin' you, she's the one! When ya know ya know. Ya know?" Hamish and Zoey were throwing each other flirtatious glances to each other across the cafe as he spoke. I looked back between my friend and Zoey and knew he was a goner. Hamish is the most lovable guy, but he falls in love with a smile. I sure hoped Zoey could handle him.

A few people started to come in for their morning coffee, so I left Zoey to her customers, grateful for all she had shared. I felt like I finally gained a small piece of the very large puzzle that was Catherine Miller. I asked Hamish if he was joining me in the bookshop but he wanted to stay and finish his coffee. Really he was going to stay and flirt with Zoey some more. I left a few dollars on the counter for my coffee and headed back to the bookshop. Catherine was busy helping a young man decide on a book so I headed upstairs to the loft ready to face Thomas.

As I walked in, Thomas was sitting at the kitchen bar with papers spread around him and his laptop open. He was quickly typing something while looking at the top document. Thomas might have been away from his office but he still had clients and cases to deal with. For all Thomas was, he was always one-hundred percent dedicated to his cases and making sure he was fully prepared for whatever might get thrown at him in the middle of court.

"Thomas."

"Michael," he responded without looking up from his work.

"Look, I meant what I said last night. I think you should go back to London. I can go through and box up the aunt's things, send you anything you'd like. I'll come home with you long enough to lay Betty and Ronnie to rest next to father but I don't think you should be here."

Thomas finally looked up from his paperwork.

"Of course, high and mighty Michael, always thinking of others instead of himself. I mean, really, where do you get off, thinking you can tell me what to do here? Telling me not to come back and help pack up our aunt's belongings."

"I'm not telling you what to do, I'm simply telling you what I think. And yes, if you want to stay and help then I'm happy for you to do that. But honestly, I figured you'd be bored here, away from work, your life back home? What's here for you?"

"You're right, Michael, nothing is here for me. But what's here for you? Or are you still thinking of that girl?" Thomas threw his hands up in defeat. "God, have it your way then. After all, this is all yours now isn't it. You get to make all the decisions. So fine, go, renew your life by appeasing that girl down there. But think about this Michael. We're all the family we have left, and while we don't always see eye to eye on things, we're still brothers and you're sending me away for some twenty-something girl that you don't even know. Our lives are in London, the firm, your company, our friends, they're all in London. You stay here and you'll be alone."

"I'm not afraid of being alone, Thomas. That's your fear."

"Fine, enjoy your lonely life then."

The tension between Thomas and I filled the room and simply would not break. Thomas shut his laptop and quickly gathered his work before he left the kitchen. First Catherine, then Thomas. Who was next? With Thomas, I had hoped it was merely his grief coming through, and his fear of being alone that caused his outburst. Regarding Catherine, well that was sheer ignorance on my part.

Hamish found his way into the bookshop an hour later. Zoey had gotten too busy to keep flirting with him. I brought him up to speed on the latest outburst and said Thomas and I were heading back to London. Hamish agreed to come back with us. He knew I would return after laying my aunts' to rest. Hamish made it clear to me that he could manage the company without me for a while, and if anything requiring my signature came up, he'd email me the details. We'd deal with it regardless of my location.

After Hamish and I made the arrangements for the three of us to return to England, I decided to try once more to convince Catherine to take the money Betty and Ronnie had left her, and hopefully get back on speaking terms before I left. As I came down to the main landing, Catherine was standing at the counter unpacking a crate of books. I gently made my presence known to her, so as not to startle her again.

"Mr. Murphy," she said when she saw me. We were back to last name usage. She looked ambivalent to seeing me. I knew I would have to explain the bet she regrettably overheard Thomas and I speaking about, she had left too fast last night for me to do so then.

"Ms. Miller," I said following her lead, "If I may, I would like to explain. You see —"

"Explain," Catherine cut me off without hesitation. "Explain how you and your brother placed a bet on me? What exactly was this bet the two of you made?"

"Please, I was ending the bet. I would never have gone through with it really, this has all been a gross misunderstanding. Thomas mistook something I said and turned it into this stupid bet, which has no bearing on... what I mean is..." I was at a loss for words with no reason for why. Catherine wasn't yelling, wasn't arguing with me, just standing there waiting for a reasonable explanation. My hope of making things right with her was looking less and less likely. I considered whether it might be better for me to stay in London and just leave this girl in peace.

"Mr. Murphy please, just tell me what the bet was?" Catherine asked frustrated.

"That Thomas could, could win you essentially. Get you to fall for him and convince you not to take the money Betty and Ronnie wanted for you." I hung my head in shame saying it aloud, I felt like a schmuck. I chanced a look at Catherine and saw nothing but disgust. I couldn't blame her. I was disgusted with my own part in the bet and for allowing Thomas to suck me into his game.

"I see." Catherine finally said after a moment. She didn't look at me but carried on, "And you thought he couldn't achieve this?"

"Pretty much," I said honestly.

"Well, at least one of you seems to have a small amount of sense, I suppose." I looked up in surprise at her comment. It seemed uncharacteristic of her given our last encounter. I expected outrage and fear not sarcasm and wit. She must have sensed my confusion as she smiled a little. "Zoey thinks you deserve a second chance. She likes you, and I agreed to try. Of course I wasn't expecting this but I gave my word and if I recall you were trying to talk Thomas out of your stupid bet?"

"Ahh yes, I called it off. Actually Thomas, Hamish and I are heading back to London tomorrow. We are taking Betty and Ronnie's ashes to lay them with our father as they requested. Thomas will not be returning so you don't have to worry about him." I hoped my news would give Catherine peace of mind and set us on a better path upon my return.

"Zoey will be disappointed. She and Hamish really hit it off." Catherine smiled and I felt that there was hope for us down the line.

"Yes, they really seem to have, don't they."

"Hope you have a safe trip, Mr. Murphy." I could see Catherine was torn between remaining cold for pride's sake and warming up to me, but it was clear she was making an effort.

"I will be returning once Thomas and I have laid them to rest and I've dealt with a few business matters. I can't make any promises for Hamish, but he seems to be rather inclined towards Zoey, I'm sure he'll find a way to stay in her life."

"Time will tell for those two I guess." Catherine said as she removed another book from the crate.

"Oh, and…" I started again, searching for the right words to change the subject. "Ms. Miller, this," handing Catherine the check, "is the promised sum from Betty and Ronnie. Please accept it along with my deepest apologies." Catherine took the check as I continued to speak. "I would like it when I return if we could possibly start over? I realize that all of this has been rather distressing and difficult for, well for us all. And I know that Betty and Ronnie loved you, and wanted nothing more than the best for you. I can see that you loved them just as much. I couldn't be happier knowing that someone cared for them when I was unable to. Please think about us starting over."

Catherine looked up from the floor and gave me a soft smile, from which I took encouragement.

"Enjoy your trip, Michael." With that, Catherine placed the check in the back pocket of her jeans then grabbed a stack of books and wandered off into the shop. My earlier conversation with Zoey ran through my mind. I had hoped, armed with a little more knowledge of Catherine, I would be able to understand her more. Yet after every conversation with her, I didn't seem to get much closer. I could tell Catherine was on the fence about me but hoped that by the time I returned from London she would be closer to making up her mind.

As I watched Catherine wander off into the stacks of books I couldn't help but wonder: Who she was? Where did she come from? I figured I'd have to live with never knowing. If she hadn't told my aunts or even Zoey, she certainly wouldn't tell me. No, I had to be content that Ms. Catherine Miller would remain a mystery to me.

CHAPTER FIVE

The Old Black Curtain

IT WAS NEARLY three weeks before I could return to Betty and Veronica's Books. Thomas and I had put our aunt's ashes to rest with our father, but we were still on icy terms. Things got slightly better back in London but for the most part, we weren't speaking. Thomas returned to work. I took the few meetings I needed and prepared to take a long leave of absence.

During my time in London I spent most of it with Mr. King, going over papers, signing the deed to Betty and Veronica's Books, and going over my own will and insurance in case anything should happen. It's odd how the loss of someone you love makes you reassess your own life, makes you want to set your own affairs in order. I also received my divorce decree. I was officially free from Robin.

By the time I was off the plane and standing in front of the bookshop, it was close to midnight. The store was closed, but Zoey Johnson was just coming out of ZZZ Up Coffee, locking up for the night.

"Oh, hey there Michael," she caught me just as I had finished unlocking the door. "You're back then. You know some of us weren't sure you or your brother or Hamish were going to come back." She continued walking over to me.

"Yeah well, I've only just arrived. I'm afraid I ended up on a rather late flight. You're here late?" I gave her a smile in return for the one on her bubbly face.

"Oh yeah, I forgot my phone when I closed up earlier... so um... did Hamish come with you or is he returning later?" Zoey asked with a hopeful tone in her voice.

"Ah no, Hamish is staying in London. One of us needs to stay there and run the company." It seemed Hamish had made quite the impression on Zoey.

"Oh, I see," she replied. I couldn't help but notice the disappointment in her voice. "Well, it's nice that you're back." Zoey shifted back to her cheerful bubbly self in a flash. "You look like you need a drink. I tend to keep a bottle behind the counter if you wanna nightcap?" Zoey offered, pointing back to the closed coffee shop.

"Maybe another night. Right now all I want is my pillow, but thank you." I smiled at the bubbly girl in thanks for her kind offer.

"Looking forward to it! Goodnight then!" Zoey waved as she said goodbye and headed off down the street. I watched her for a second or two before heading inside the shop. I was too tired and jet-lagged to think of anything but sleep. I dropped my bags at the entrance of the loft, found my way to bed, and tried not to think about all the work I had ahead of me.

I woke the following morning to a knock and the smell of coffee. I emerged from the bedroom, still in my clothes from the night before. I wandered over to the knocking, sliding the loft door open to find Catherine standing there holding two cups of coffee and a paper bag.

"Morning" I said, slightly hoarse from just waking up.

"Morning. Zoey said you got in kind of late last night. I thought you might want… well breakfast?" Catherine gestured to the coffee and bag in her hands.

"Thank you," I said taking one of the coffees and stepped aside, letting Catherine pass me. I watched her as she went into the kitchen, placing her coffee and the bag on the kitchen bar. As she moved around the kitchen I realised she knew her way around it. She grabbed us a couple of plates and placed them on the counter. Then she pulled two breakfast sandwiches and some hash browns out of the bag and started unwrapping everything, putting it on the plates. She pushed one of the plates in front of me as I took a seat on the bar stool. Catherine sat down and smiled slightly. Thankful for the breakfast she provided, as well as her company, I smiled back.

"My way of saying welcome back and let's start over." As she spoke, I could tell she was still a tad wary but had let go of what had passed between us and was willing to start anew. Catherine and I had our breakfast mostly in silence. We exchanged basic pleasantries but nothing of great consequence. It was nice. I cleaned up after breakfast; it seemed only right as Catherine had provided the food and coffee. Catherine went downstairs to open up the shop.

I felt refreshed after a shower and some clean clothes. I was pleased to be getting a second chance with Catherine and was determined not to squander it. As Catherine tended to the shop, I started going through all of my aunt's belongings. I started with the few things I knew Thomas would want and set them aside to send to him. However, I really had no idea what to do with the majority of their things.

By Friday, I had managed to organize the whole loft. I separated what to trash, and what to donate. I sorted out which little keepsakes I wanted, as well as some for Thomas. I'll say this about Betty and Ronnie, they were pack-rats. They seemed to have kept everything. After hours of sorting, I was dying for a drink only to discover I had completely run out of booze. It had been almost a full twenty-four hours since I'd even stepped outside, I needed some fresh air. Remembering Zoey had a tendency to keep a bottle behind the counter of the coffee shop, I decided to see if she was still next door and up for a nightcap.

I stood outside in the brisk cool air, breathing deeply and felt refreshed. I walked over to ZZZ Up Coffee to find it completely locked up, I didn't know offhand of any other place to get a nightcap and was almost content with merely calling it a night when I heard music. It was faint and a little ways away but it was there, and where there is music, one can usually find a drink. So I followed the music.

It didn't take me long to locate where the music was coming from, it was coming from a little side alley. When I turned into the alley, I noticed a nook with about four steps going down, leading to a white door that was partially covered with a draped black curtain tied off to the right side.

I headed down the dark steps and entered. It took a few moments for my eyes to adjust, but once they did, I felt as though I had gone back in time. The whole place looked as if it were still the 1950's. Round tables were set around the main floor area, with space at the front for dancing, and a platform stage where a band was set up. They were playing Bing Crosby's 'Jazz, Jazz, Jazz' from his film 'High Society'. I recognized the song immediately. My father had been a huge Bing Crosby fan and to tell you the truth, so was I. Enjoying Bing Crosby with him were some of the few good memories I had of my father. We would often sit together and listen to old crooner music. My father had the complete Crosby collection, which I later happily inherited. Now, in this mysterious nightclub, I immediately felt right at home.

The place was quiet except for a few patrons at their tables while the rest were empty. The subtle sweet aroma of whiskey and scotch tinged the air as I scanned the room looking for a good place to sit. I noticed the bar along the right side of the club. I wandered over to order a drink and continued to take in my new surroundings.

"Macallan neat, thanks," I said to the bartender when he asked what I was drinking. As he poured my drink I asked him what this place was all about.

"The Old Black Curtain," he replied, handing me my drink.

"Like a place out of time," I voiced.

"Yeah, built in the 1950s but over the years it's been updated without losing its original feel. We have some in-house bands and three or four regular singers who rotate through the week. The bands plays blues and jazz Mondays,

Wednesdays and Saturdays. Newer contemporary tunes on Tuesdays and Thursdays. Fridays and Sundays are pretty much a free for all. The band and the singer that's scheduled can play whatever they like. Most of the girls tend to do some of their original stuff. You showed up at a good time, our most popular singer is about to start." When I reached for my wallet to pay, the bartender asked, "Wanna start a tab?" I agreed and took a seat at a small table tucked away in the corner.

The corner table was a bit shadowy but allowed a perfect view of the stage. With my back against the brick wall, I could see the entrance and exit from the corner of my eye. It was perfect. The band finished playing out their song and moved into the next. As they played the intro, what little light was on the stage went out as a spotlight moved to centre stage and the singer found her first note. As she sang, I couldn't believe what I was witnessing. It was Catherine, singing Billie Holiday's 'God Bless the Child'. It was without a doubt the sweetest sound I had ever heard. Listening to her sing was like standing at the gates of heaven waiting to be welcomed in. I didn't even know that was possible. Catherine Miller stood on that stage with more confidence than I had ever seen from her, and once the applause ended, she moved on to her next song, 'The Falling Leaves.' I was enraptured again as she sang with such poise and grace. I never wanted her to stop. I tore my eyes from the stage for a moment to look at the audience. Catherine's voice seemed to relax everyone sitting in the club, no one spoke, no one made a sound as she sang her heart out. From 'The Falling

Leaves' she moved into 'It Had to Be You'. Time seemed to stop with every note.

Having feared that she was nothing more than a very cautious, quiet young woman, I was thrilled to see this side of Catherine. Looking around the club at the other patrons, I noticed how every one of them focused on Catherine. I had never seen someone control an entire room with nothing more than a song. Catherine's voice was like honey, soft and smooth. She moved on to sing Doris Day's 'Autumn Leaves' and I turned my attention to her again. Looking at Catherine in her lovely floor-length green silk dress singing those jazz classics, I was thoroughly enchanted.

I couldn't remember the last time I had a better evening. I was in heaven that night, listening to Catherine. But I recalled Zoey's warning, to take my time and let Catherine have her space. She was already cautious around me, I didn't want to overwhelm her again. Her last song for the night was one I'd never heard before, and it took me a moment to realize it was probably one of her own.

> *'There are challenges ahead of me*
> *But I know I'll make it through*
> *Life is nothing but a story*
> *That the light shines through*
>
> *I am building my story*
> *Stepping out from the page*
> *I throw the book away*
> *And follow the path laid before me*

Though the rain falls
And drowns me
I take the rain and grow strong
My heart will guide me
On my journey
Cause I know, I know I'll make it one day

There are challenges ahead of me
And I know the road is long
And I may fail and make many mistakes
But I know I'll be okay

I'll fly, like a mockingbird
I'll soar higher than none can see
I'll find my freedom, on my journey
Cause I know, oh I know
I know I'll make it one day

There are challenges ahead of me
I am building my story'

I left The Old Black Curtain that night with Catherine's sweet angelic voice filling my mind, hopelessly anticipating the next time I could hear her sing. Catherine's voice carried me off to sleep that night.

The next morning when Catherine came into the shop I wanted to confess seeing her at The Old Black Curtain, but I hesitated. Catherine and I were finally getting to know each other and we were making progress. I didn't want to jeopardize the friendship we were slowly forming. Her guard was slowly but surely coming down around me and I hoped that one day she would be comfortable enough around me to be as open as she had been with Betty and Ronnie, or even with Zoey. I knew we were nowhere near that yet, though. I had decided that getting to know Catherine was a long-term goal.

I returned to The Old Black Curtain nearly every night since first finding it. Soon I became a regular, and Raymond the bartender started giving me my Macallan before I'd even ask for it. That corner became my corner, it was open every time I walked in. I would sit there night after night with my drink, waiting in anticipation for Catherine to step into the spotlight. She would sing and soften the hearts of every patron in The Old Black Curtain. She had a wonderful range of songs to choose from. Songs from Frank, Bing, Cole, Holiday, Clooney, Monroe, and so many more. I became addicted to hearing her, watching her be who I felt she was meant to be up on that stage. It was the only place she didn't seem to hide, where, perhaps, she couldn't hide. It was sheer beauty.

This went on for two weeks, working with Catherine during the day in the shop, slowly going through all of my aunt's possessions, then watching her sing at night, all the while not saying a word about The Old Black Curtain. I had created a routine, going through one box, one room at a time. Dragging out the process as long as possible to take up more time, extend my usefulness as such. In the afternoons I would head down to the shop, have Catherine show me the ins and outs of everything. Regrettably, this did not take as much time as I had hoped. Running the shop was far easier than the multi-billion dollar company Hamish and I had created. Ensure the parts, in this case books, arrived on schedule, log them, then put them out on the floor. The ancient cash register was simple enough to get the hang of and the few customers we'd see in a day mostly paid by debit or credit, so there was very little cash to actually handle. On the night's Catherine sang at The Old Black Curtain, I would sit in my corner and watch her dazzle the audience. Catherine never mentioned if she had seen me there.

It wasn't until my third week in that things started to change, when our lives changed. It was like any other night at The Old Black Curtain. I was sitting at my usual table with a drink. Catherine was just finishing up her fourth song, Billie Holiday's 'The Very Thought of You'. She took a sip of water as the band gently started to play the next song, which happened to be one of her originals.

'I've been locked up in this tower
For so many years
Waiting for you to come and break my chains
I had so many dreams
Before I was locked away
Know all I can do is wait

Then I can be free
From this prison I am in
I can be free
From this torturous dream
Can't you see this girl
Locked up and alone
Wishing for better, wishing for a home'

As Catherine sang I felt as if it meant something more. It was as though she was singing with more soul than usual.

> *'I stand alone at night*
> *And wish upon the stars*
> *That you would find me locked away*
> *I don't know when*
> *And I don't know how*
> *But I believe that you*
> *Would come for me*
>
> *I try to dream of angels*
> *And all the pretty things*
> *Like princes and knights*
> *And fairy-tales*
>
> *Then I can be free*
> *From this prison I am in*
> *I can be free*
> *From this torturous dream*
> *Can't you see this girl*
> *Locked up and alone*
> *Can't you see this girl*
> *Locked up and alone*
> *Wishing for better, wishing for a home*
> *Wishing for better, wishing for a home'*

When Catherine finished, she disappeared off-stage and the musicians started to play Frank Sinatra's, 'For Once in My Life.' I had finished my drink and was about to head home when Raymond, put another down in front of me.

"Compliments from the lady," Raymond said before heading back towards the bar.

"Lady? What lady?" I asked while looking around the club.

"This lady!" Catherine said, as she put her drink down on the table and sat down. I was stunned, what was she doing at my table? Before taking a sip from her drink, and with eyes fixed on me, she said, "Enjoying the show, Mr. Murphy?"

She seemed different somehow, more confident and sure. Her demeanour was as though she was still on stage, nothing like the way she conducted herself in the bookshop. In there, she's quiet, mostly keeps to herself, even when we speak she scarcely glances my way. Catherine was clearly more comfortable in The Old Black Curtain. I had never seen her more relaxed than at that moment. Catherine continued to surprise me.

"Oh yes, very much," I replied after a moment, and suddenly curious as to where the evening might take us. Curious as to whether or not I might actually learn something more about her.

"How long have you known I've been coming here?" I asked.

"Oh, I saw you sitting here one night and asked Raymond. He mentioned you had been showing up every so often."

"You never said anything?"

"Well, neither did you and I was still unsure about you but now... now I don't know, I guess you're not so bad." She smiled and my heart melted. As cold and closed off as

Catherine seemed to be, it didn't matter anymore. I had convinced her I was safe and trustworthy.

We stayed for a while, keeping the conversation fairly light. Once our drinks were finished, Catherine stood.

"I have to grab my bag from the green room, will you walk me home?" Catherine asked so sweetly.

"Of course" I responded instantly, standing from the table.

I followed Catherine past the stage and down the shadowy brick-walled hall. The rest of the building wasn't much, a few rooms and the back exit. Catherine led me to the second door on the right. The green room was small but spacious, with a dark carpet, two loveseats facing each other, and a table between them. A mirror covered the entire right wall and there was a long table sitting beneath it.

Catherine walked straight to the table. She gathered her hairbrush, make-up and a few hairpins and tossed them in a small bag. She tossed the make-up bag into her large purse hanging off the back of a chair.

"So I've decided that I can trust you." She stated as a matter of fact, turning to face me.

"Really?" I was confounded as I stood before her.

"Really." She was being playful again.

In her little black and silver evening dress with the mirror behind her, I could see most of her back. I took another step towards her and said,

"I'm glad."

"Good." She said with a smile. We were standing inches from each other now as she took another step closer. I could almost feel her.

"Just... don't hurt me?" she breathed, her lips almost touching mine. Her words threw me for a second. I figured this was a girl who had been hurt in the past and was just trying to make sure it wouldn't happen again.

"Never." I said, and as the words escaped my lips, she inched closer still. I placed my hands on the sides of her waist cautiously, not sure how she would react. She didn't stop me, she didn't back away. Instead, Catherine wrapped her arms around my neck as our lips finally touched. After a second, our kiss grew deeper. We scarcely stopped for breath, engrossed in each other. I found myself wanting more of her, wanting her closer. We fell onto the dressing table as our kiss, and mutual desire took over.

CHAPTER SIX

Settle Down

OVER AND OVER, I found myself replaying that intimate moment Catherine and I shared in the green room. It consumed my every waking thought. In one brief moment, I had experienced more passion, more excitement than in my entire marriage to Robin. I was beyond hooked, and I knew I wanted nothing more than to be with Catherine. The more time we spent together, the more I wanted to know her past, her story. I also knew she'd never tell me. Since our first meeting, I had learned only a little about her, but I wasn't about to botch it up now. There was no prying, no pressing her to share. If I learned anything, it was that Catherine Miller was a private person and would not reveal more than she wished. It took another two weeks after I got back, just to convince her to accept the $20,000 from Aunt Betty and Aunt Ronnie. When I returned from London, I saw the cheque still sitting under the cash register.

Catherine consumed my every thought, and I couldn't help but imagine where our kiss would have led had we not been interrupted. The bass player walked in and the three of us awkwardly stood there in the green room, none of us knowing what to say. Catherine grabbed her bag off the back of the chair as we mumbled awkward apologies and headed straight for the exit. I walked Catherine home, in silent tension most of the way.

I was amazed how short the walk was from The Old Back Curtain to Catherine's home. Catherine mentioned she and Zoey were roommates, unaware that Zoey had told me the day after Betty and Ronnie's funeral. We turned another corner and arrived at a large two-storied Victorian style house. It had been left to Zoey by her grandmother.

Looking at the house, with its gable roof, arched stained glass windows and wrap-around porch, was like stepping back to the nineteenth century. Painted a deep teal with the elaborate gingerbread trim in white, the house was rather delightful. I thought it a shame no one built homes like this anymore.

As I walked Catherine up to her front door, the slightly worn porch creaked. I stood there, wanting her in my arms again, craving the feel of her lips on mine. I was trying to read her, waiting for some gesture or hint, but it seemed the magical passion from earlier had faded. Catherine gently kissed my cheek, saying goodnight before heading inside, leaving me on her battered porch. Nevertheless, a thrill stirred through me, anticipating our next meeting.

The next time I saw Catherine, it didn't go as I had hoped. She seemed to have retreated, somewhat, behind her wall again. I am thankful it was only somewhat. She started to come over early so we could share breakfast. Some mornings she'd cook, others I did. Eventually, she started staying late and we'd have dinner before heading over to The Old Black Curtain. It quickly became our thing, looking up new recipes to try. Some worked, some did not. At the club, Catherine and I would sit at my table and have a drink before her set. When the night was over, I would walk her home, and at the front door, she would say goodnight, giving me a light kiss on the cheek.

Our pace was slow but steady and I didn't mind one bit. After all, still fresh in my mind was my failed marriage, and I knew the only way things would work with Catherine was to let her set the pace. The weeks rolled on and we were happy. With each passing day, Catherine let her guard down a little more. I knew spontaneity was out of the question with Catherine as she was very structured, very routine, yet she was adaptable. No matter what was thrown at her in a day, she could handle each situation with diplomacy, quickly thinking to find solutions and keeping a cool head in the process. The more time we spent together, the more I admired all that she was.

We talked at length about our favourite books and musicians. We often discussed Jane Austen's *Northanger Abbey*, how and why she strongly connected with the heroine, Catherine Morland. She loved how that character wasn't held back from her imagination even though it sometimes got her into trouble. It shaped her overall character, made her who she was meant to be. Catherine told me she found comfort in the character's silly naive notions and innocent beliefs, almost as if she envied them. Catherine rarely went anywhere without her copy of *Northanger Abbey*, it seemed to be a security blanket of sorts. We spoke of music, our favourite artists (we both loved Bing), and how she dreamed of singing with the same feeling and emotion as Billie Holiday. She loved singing jazz standards more than anything else. She would always sing along whenever we watched a musical.

As close as we became, she still wouldn't tell me about her family, her life before Victoria. I wanted, so badly, for her to tell me. I wanted to know all of her, but she was still keeping me at a distance. I was almost resigned to the idea of never knowing Catherine's story, but once again she surprised me.

It was a night like any other. We were sitting at our table in The Old Black Curtain, and the band was on stage playing Frank Sinatra's 'That's Life' when Catherine suddenly started talking, her eyes were closed as she gently swayed to the song.

"Mmm, I love this one," she said softly. "I used to have a friend back in Toronto who would play it for me whenever I was down," she said and opened her eyes.

"Oh, you've been there? That's where I'm from actually… before moving to Scotland for school," I said, thrilled she was sharing.

"It's where I'm from too." Catherine smiled and took another sip from her Southside. "I pretty much hitchhiked my way over here."

"What made you come here?" I asked cautiously hoping she would reveal more.

"I used to sing in a club, much like this one. It was all I knew, all there was but you reach a point in life when you have to make a change. You don't know if it's going to be good or bad, you just have to follow wherever it leads."

Catherine finished her drink as she stood from the table. She gave me a soft kiss and told me she needed to get ready for her set. As she walked away, I mulled over her words: *you have to make a change.* She was right, the world doesn't change. We change.

Catherine took the stage and sang three standards before she changed it up with one of her own.

> *'Love, I never knew*
> *Love, I never sought*
> *Love, I never felt, I never dreamed*
> *Ohhhh*
>
> *Till you caught me and pulled me from my tomb*
> *Oh you taught me, to ease this damaged soul*
> *Oh you changed me, to see life anew*
> *Oh you saved me, so I could breathe with you'*

Catherine's voice faded and the band played on. A heavy bass line set in over the piano and Catherine closed her eyes, moving slightly to the melody. Her voice came in again, and she poured her soul into the song:

> *'I learned to shy away, too afraid to play the fool*
> *Content to be alone, till you walked through*
> *my door*

Oh cause you caught me, and healed this
broken girl
Oh you taught me, the meaning of a home
Oh you changed me, with a joy and hope
Oh love you saved me, so I can breathe with you'

When Catherine finished singing, it looked as though she wiped a tear away before beginning Margaret Whiting's 'My Foolish Heart'. She looked beautiful and alive, bearing her soul for all to hear in each note. I didn't know what made her tear-up singing her original song, but I was honoured to witness it. Catherine carried on with her set, transitioning to Rosemary Clooney's 'Love, You Didn't Do Right By Me.' As I listened I noticed a theme, every song was about love. Experiencing it, being hurt by it, losing it. I wondered if Catherine had ever been in love. I had been toying with the idea of telling her that I loved her, but in the right way, with the right words. Honestly, a part of me couldn't shake the feeling that she wouldn't be receptive to my declaration. After all, Catherine never reacted the way I expected, that's part of what made me love her. Then her words came back to mind: *"You reach a point in life when you have to make a change. You don't know if it's going to be good or bad, you just have to follow wherever it leads."*

It was another piece of her riddle-filled life I was slowly coming to know. Of course, we all want change. We all strive for something different in our lives and in the midst of that change we don't always know if it's for better or worse, but either way, we have to endure it.

As Catherine performed, a man walked in. I had never seen him there before. Keeping to the back wall near the bar, he was scanning the room. He didn't interest me much, not until I saw his reaction to seeing Catherine. He looked angry, with clenched fists at his sides, ready to knock someone about. The man was tall, maybe six foot and slender, with visible muscle. I could see a number of tattoos on him, a black raven on his neck really stood out. With short sandy brown hair, he stood strong and tough, definitely not a man to cross. For a moment the stranger had my full attention, however, Catherine's angelic voice pulled my eyes away from him and back to the stage.

Catherine finished up the song, and when the music dwindled to a soft hum she did something unexpected. For the first time since I had been going to The Old Black Curtain, Catherine introduced her next song:

"This last one tonight is for someone very close to me." Her voice was a little shaky, unused to actually speaking on stage. As the music started, I knew it was one of her originals again, only this time she seemed to be giving her heart away.

> *'It's said home where your heart is*
> *But if your heart can't settle down*
> *It's been hardened for a fool*
> *Pushed under by blood torn*
> *So how will I know I'm home*
> *Ohh ohh oh*
>
> *Now I've started over*
> *More times than I can count*
> *And when I think I've hit rock bottom*
> *I found it went further down*
> *So how will I know I'm home*

And I keep running,
Miles and miles,
But my heart couldn't settle
Not till you, not till you came around

Oh, when you feel it, when you're overwhelmed
Do you surrender the fight, do you stir
and breathe
When you know you're home
ohhh --- ohh

And I keep running
Miles and miles
But my heart couldn't settle down
Not till you, not till you came around
'Cause it's said home is where your heart is
But not till you came around'

She finished and headed offstage. It was then that I remembered the stranger. I looked around to see if he was still in the room, but didn't see him. So I just sat there, waiting for Catherine to return and have a drink with me before taking her home. Raymond brought our drinks after Catherine's set finished. After a few minutes, I wondered what was taking so long. When she finally made her way to the table, the man I'd noticed earlier walked out of the club, clearly in a huff. I focused my attention on Catherine as she downed her drink in one. She looked as though she had seen a ghost, her face was pale and her eyes a little red. I wondered if she had been crying.

"Everything all right?" I asked with concern.

"Take me home." Catherine said. She stood, grabbed her bag off the back of the chair, and headed out. I followed, leaving my half-finished drink on the table.

Catherine didn't say a word as I escorted her home. As we walked, Catherine took my arm, tucking into me. She didn't let go, even after we were standing before the front door. I was waiting for her usual goodnight kiss before she went in, but she didn't go inside. Instead she stood there, holding my hands and staring at me.

"Catherine, are you alright?" I struggled to contain the worry I was feeling. She closed her hazel-green eyes and I watched as tears fell. I desperately wanted her to confide in me, to let me help. I wanted to carry some of her burdens if only she'd let down her walls long enough to let me.

"You won't hurt me, will you Michael?" she asked as she looked at me through tear-filled eyes. I let go of her hands to brush a tear from her cheek. Then, gently taking her chin in my hand, I simply said, "Never."

Our lips found each other quickly and it was like our first kiss all over again. I pulled Catherine close and our kiss grew deeper. She broke away, but only for a moment to catch her breath. Then she turned to open her front door and lead me inside. The house was dark, not a single light on, but Catherine knew her way around. She dropped her bag on the small table beside the door. I moved behind, wrapping my arms around her petite waist as my lips found the base of her neck. Catherine turned to face me and our lips met briefly before she turned, leading me down the hallway and upstairs.

When we made it to her bedroom she turned on a lamp and I caught a glimpse of the soft emerald green walls of the room before she distracted me again. She leaned in for another kiss as her arms wrapped around my torso. My fingers found the back of her dress, undoing the top button and gliding the zipper all the way down, then her dress fell to the floor. Catherine's hands found the buttons on my shirt and I waited in anticipation as she undid each one. I lifted her in my arms and as her legs wrapped around my hips and I walked us over to her bed. Catherine hadn't said what upset her earlier but I no longer cared. All I wanted was the warmth of her, and the scent of her soft lavender-mint perfume I loved. Finally, I had the woman of my dreams in my arms. I savoured every moment.

We lay wrapped in each other's arms, tired but not ready for sleep. Catherine was resting her head on my chest as I sat up, leaning against the headboard. She made my heart sing. Being with her, I finally understood what had been missing in my marriage to Robin and it was passion and respect, a bond between equals. I knew Catherine was still full of secrets and barriers but none of that worried me. Whatever they were, however dark her past might be, I was determined to make sure that her future held nothing but love and joy.

As Catherine leaned against me, her body pressed against mine felt so right, so natural. She softly whispered, "I love you. You make me less afraid." With a smile, she shifted enough to kiss me then settled herself back down, nestling into me. I pulled her close, willing her fears away. I never wanted to wake from this dream. "I love you too," I whispered before we both drifted off to sleep.

CHAPTER SEVEN

Haunted

I WANTED TO keep my eyes shut tight. I was warm and cozy with Catherine lightly weighing on my chest. I could not remember the last time I had felt so content. As the bright sunlight of a new day came shining through the windows, I could not sleep any longer. Catherine rolled over into her pillow, and I took a moment to admire her beauty as she slept, unaffected by the morning light. I sat up in her four-poster queen bed and let my eyes take in the room.

It was large, with lots of open space. The left wall had two open doors, one was her closet that appeared to be a walk-in, and the other, a bathroom. The wall opposite had double stained-glass doors leading out to a balcony. Nearby sat an electric keyboard and in the corner, her small-bodied guitar. The wall adjacent to the bed had two overflowing bookcases and a desk in between them. There was a television mounted on the wall above the desk for perfect viewing from the bed.

Catherine shifted onto her stomach with her head facing me on her pillow. I smiled as I brushed her hair from her face. My touch stirred her and she slowly opened her eyes.

"Morning," she breathed a few seconds later, before sitting up.

"Good morning," I said with a grin, tucking a stray hair behind her ear.

"Mmmm, scruffy," she said while running a hand over the stubble on my jaw. "You ever think of shaving? Bet you'd look ten years younger clean-shaven." Catherine smiled and leaned in to kiss me again.

"Don't like the scruff? Is that what you are trying to tell me?" I teased between kisses.

I love the scruff. It was more of a wonder than anything." She yawned, rubbing the sleep from her eyes. "What time is it?"

"A little after seven, we have some time before we have to go to the shop." I kissed her forehead, thinking about her comment about my scruff.

"Breakfast?" Catherine asked with a smile.

"Ya, breakfast sounds good," I said as Catherine hopped out of bed, throwing on her blue cotton robe on the way to the bathroom. I grabbed my clothes off the bedroom floor and re-dressed, figuring I'd change when I got back to the shop. I heard the water running and Catherine called out:

"I'm just gonna have a quick shower. Feel free to go downstairs and look at what you want for breakfast. Be down in a few."

"Okay." I answered, before heading out to find the kitchen.

The hallway was a wide rectangle, with the staircase on the right and three doors leading to other rooms. The walls were a light lavender shade with white wainscotting on the lower portion. I headed down the stairs, admiring a couple of paintings Zoey and Catherine had hung. I paused to look closer at one. It was a 19th-century clipper ship in the middle of the sea, with the sun setting behind it. I thought it was great, and when I looked for the artist's name in the bottom right-hand corner, I was surprised to see it was Zoey's. She was an exquisite painter. I glanced at the others and sure enough, they were Zoey's. Overall, the house was lovely, light and airy. I noticed a few more of Zoey's paintings hanging in the main hallway, then I came across an arched opening leading to the living room, with a couple of stairs at the far end leading down to the kitchen. The same light lavender shade covered the walls, and the floor was a rich mahogany hardwood.

I found my way to a bathroom on the main floor. I freshened up, running water over my face. Looking at my stubbly grey beard, I considered whether it was time to shave. It had been a while. I thought about Catherine's comment about how much younger I would look. I had never worried about my appearance — as I'd been grey from such an early age it never occurred to me that I looked older.

Back in the kitchen, I started to look through the fridge for something to cook. I settled on omelettes, with toast and orange juice. I was pouring eggs into the frying pan when Catherine appeared. Dressed in an emerald-green sundress and strappy black sandals, her braided hair entwined into a bun, she looked happy and rested.

"Mmm... something smells good," she started, "Oh! Wow!" Catherine said as she looked at me.

"You know you didn't have to shave, right? It was just a passing comment. I did like what you had going on there." She chuckled taking a sip from a glass of orange juice.

"I know, I decided it was time, that's all."

"Hmm, I was right though. Adorable, simply adorable," she said kissing my freshly shaved cheek.

"Except the grey though?" I said and leaned into her touch while keeping an eye on my frying omelette.

"No, I like the grey. Makes you look wise and worldly." She wrapped her arms around me as she watched me cook. "Looks good."

"Should be ready in a minute or two," I said as the toaster popped. Before I could reach the toast, Catherine let go of me, grabbed it and started to butter the two pieces as I finished the omelette. As we ate our breakfast, I couldn't help but feel how comfortable Catherine and I had become. I was truly happy, and Catherine made me believe she was as well.

The four months went by quickly, but they could not have been better. I had become a part of Catherine's life, from employer to friend to lover. Eventually, we spent nearly every night together. We were at The Old Black Curtain on the nights she sang. We had created a routine that fit both our lives quite easily. I was still managing M&M Tech with Hamish. He had come back for two weeks to visit, but Catherine and I knew he really only came to see Zoey. They had managed to make the long-distance thing work between them. He had flown out to visit at least once a month since they met and for one very long weekend, Hamish had surprised Zoey with a plane ticket to visit him in London.

When he was here, Hamish and I talked about the possibility of opening a third branch in Victoria, the place where both our hearts lay but we had to run it past our board and figure out who would manage the London branch. We also discussed whether Catherine and Zoey would be interested in moving to London. That would mean selling the bookshop and settling back home, but I knew how much Catherine loved the shop and The Old Black Curtain. I wasn't so sure she'd want to move. Hamish was convinced Zoey would go in a heartbeat. While she was visiting him there, Hamish said she simply loved the ambience and culture of London. For the time being, we let it be. The two women in our lives were happy and M&M Tech was flourishing. We had no reason to broach the subject with them yet.

The man with the black raven tattoo returned to The Old Black Curtain. He showed up more often until he appeared at least twice a week. Every time he came he would stay in the shadows of the club, watching Catherine. After a while of this, I decided to ask Catherine if she knew him, but instead of answering she changed the subject. I wasn't sure exactly what it was about this strange man, but I knew I didn't like him. Always watching Catherine, but I couldn't say anything, Catherine was not about to talk about him. So whatever she knew or was keeping from me, I just had to accept it, and keep a close eye on him.

I had pretty well completely lost touch with my old life. Everything before Catherine, before Betty and Veronica's Books, was a blur with the exception of Hamish. I had no interest in all the messages I had been receiving from London. Most were from Thomas but I had nothing to say to him. Hamish had kept the Board of Directors off my back for as long as he could, but my long absence away was noticed. I was going to have to deal with my life in London sooner, rather than later; but for the first time in my life I was in a place that truly felt like home. I had found love and friends and felt like part of a community. I wasn't sure I was ready to leave any of it or if I would ever be ready to leave.

Of course, I had finished sorting out my aunts' belongings and the bookshop months before. I shipped a couple of boxes to Thomas with things I knew he'd like to have. I kept Betty's copy of Jane Eyre and Ronnie's square glass decanter engraved with her favourite flower, a rose. I remembered having that decanter engraved for Ronnie. I was eighteen, just about to head off to college and wanting to give her a gift I knew she would always use, and think of me when she did. Catherine kept Ronnie's blue silk scarf and Betty's wide-brimmed black fedora and helped me pack up the rest of their clothes for donation to a local charity. I left some of their private book collection to the shop and donated the rest to the city library.

I was struggling, trying to decide what to do. Every time I thought of the future, I thought of Catherine. I had completely run out of reasons to stay except for Catherine. Hamish and I were still working out a plan to either open a branch of M&M Tech in Victoria or ask Zoey and Catherine to move to London. I wondered: *Would she consider coming to England with me? Was she willing to pack up her whole life and leave?* Too many thoughts were crowding my mind, but I knew I had to make a decision — my colleagues were growing impatient.

While I was mulling over my life choices, our routine stayed the same; Betty and Veronica's, The Old Black Curtain, and spending time with Zoey. Really, the only part of my new life that bothered me was the stranger that kept watching Catherine. I was sure they knew each other. I tried not to let my imagination run wild with possibilities about their acquaintance, but it was difficult. Who was he? *Her father, her brother, an ex-lover?*

Though we had never actually met, I felt the tattooed man and I shared a common dislike for each other. Judging by the look in his eyes on some nights, I could have sworn he wanted to kill me. He seemed to be nearly twice my size and I knew I could never take him on. I doubted Hamish could even take him. I knew one thing for sure, he had eyes for Catherine. His dark eyes were constantly on her as if she somehow belonged to him. I needed Hamish, when he was back in town, to suss out the situation and help me decide what to do. Of course, Hamish might only run his mouth off to the guy. Then we'd likely both end up dead.

Catherine had grown tense since the man's arrival. I wanted to confront the guy, to find out just what he was up to and tell him to go back to wherever he came from but the thought of upsetting Catherine stopped me every time. She seemed to get more and more stressed every time he came around. I didn't intend to add to it. I felt bound to protect her. I just wasn't sure what I was trying to protect her from. All I knew of Catherine was what she had told me two months earlier. She had come quite a way in confiding in me but I couldn't help but want more. I told myself I had to be patient, and remember that with Catherine everything happens in stages, and in surprising ways. No doubt learning her life story would follow suit.

One night she finally let me in. It must have been about two in the morning when we were in bed and she gently kissed my lips and nudged me awake. The second time she kissed me, I kissed her back while wrapping my arms around her and flipping her onto her back. She smiled and continued our kiss before telling me why she had woken me.

"Michael, can I play you something?"

I wasn't quick enough to hide my surprise, telling her she could always play me something. She climbed out of bed long enough to grab her guitar before settling back down ready to play. I wiped the sleep from my eyes and sat up against the headboard. Catherine sat on the bed balancing the guitar on her knee. Playing a solid strum of every chord, she started to sing:

> *'I thought my life was over*
> *That the rain would drown me*
> *You were supposed to be my protector*
> *My everything*
> *You charmed me with your lies*
> *Charmed me with your promises*

Now I'm haunted
By the memory of you
I'm haunted
By the things that you do
I try to run away, hide from you
But I'm still haunted
By you'

Catherine's rhythm picked up a bit as she was strumming and singing full out now.

'I thought I could start over
But I couldn't find a way
Forget the painful past and move on
But you followed me
You couldn't let me go

Now I'm haunted
By the memory of you
I'm haunted
By the things that you do
I try to run away, hide from you
But I'm still haunted

Know I've found my love, my happiness
My past can lay to rest
I don't cry over you cause that stage is through
I'm stronger, I'm stronger,
I'm stronger than you

Now I'm not haunted
By the memory of you
I'm not haunted
By the things that you do
I don't need to run away,
Or hide from you
You don't own me, you can't control me
I won't get haunted, I won't get haunted,
I won't get haunted
By you'

Catherine looked over at me and I was speechless. Her song held so much. If she truly felt haunted by her life, it's no wonder she kept to herself. I wouldn't open up easily either. I wiped a small tear away from the corner of my eye as Catherine put her guitar away and sat down on the edge of the bed. I found myself struggling to find the right words to say. Her song revealed a significant part of her life story, and all I wanted to do was be as supportive as possible. I felt honoured she finally felt comfortable enough with me to share her feelings and some of her past struggles. I was seeing a part of the real Catherine, the part that she kept hidden away.

"That was beautiful," I said as I reached for her hand and kissed it. I could feel Catherine relax and take a deep breath. Her eyes told me everything. She wanted to confide in me, in someone, but fear was holding her back. Catherine closed her eyes, taking another breath. She slowly shook her head and said:

"I… I don't even know where to begin… how to begin," she said, in a soft, vulnerable voice. Her tears began falling and I moved across the bed, taking her in my arms. She had started crying and couldn't seem to stop. All I did was hold her as she cried, wanting her to feel safe with me. There would be no judgment, no pressure from me for any explanation. I have no idea how long we sat there like that, and I didn't care.

Eventually, Catherine stopped crying and opened her eyes. I knew she was ready to fill me in on her past. She sat cross-legged on the bed and leaned back against the headboard. I leaned back and quietly waited for her to begin.

"Well, as you know, I grew up in Toronto. My father raised my brother and I pretty much on his own. I never knew my mother. My father told me she died in childbirth with me. Peter, my brother, is three years older and was always in charge when dad wasn't around. He owned a nightclub and that was basically our playground. He was always at the club and when Peter and I were not in school we were there too.

"The thing you have to understand about the club is that it had two purposes: the front end was a club like any other, very similar to The Old Black Curtain, where people sat around drinking and listening to the acts that came through. The back end, however, was where he really made his money. Dad had converted the underbelly of the business into an illegal brothel, and it did very well. His place was one everyone knew about but no one talked about. My father had a high ranking police officer on his payroll which kept the police out of his business."

Her voice dripped with shame at the mention of her father's business. I couldn't even imagine what her childhood would have been like growing up in that environment.

"By the time Peter was fifteen, our father started teaching him how the business worked and Peter took right to it. He had no problem following dad's example. Me, I didn't have the stomach for it and wanted nothing to do with the business, so I kept to the nightclub. I had a good ear for music and picked up songs quickly. By the time I was ten, I had taught myself piano, with some help from a few of the musicians that played in the club. I learned all their songs. When I was fourteen, dad decided I was old enough to work in the club. Mostly as a busser, sometimes as a server if he was short-staffed, and every so often I'd get to sing with the band.

"I didn't mind working in the club really, it didn't interfere with my school or anything and it kept me busy. Dad didn't pay me much though. The staff would slip me tips from time to time when he wasn't around, they were great! Encouraging me with each song I sang and teaching me how to work a crowd, a table. They gave me life skills and a sense of family outside of my father and brother. Of course, they knew about the backroom business my father was running, but as long as it didn't touch the lounge and they got paid, they all kept quiet.

"My issues with my father, my brother, didn't start up until I was about fifteen. I grew up... well I mean, I grew into a pretty young woman and when I was fifteen my father decided... he forced me to... to work in the brothel."

Catherine choked up as she forced the words out. She paused for a moment to wipe tears from her eyes. I could see this was hard for her to talk about, and I could understand why. As I sat listening, I wanted to scream, to curse any man who would, who could do that to his own daughter. What kind of man saw his daughter as a dollar sign instead of the beautiful, gifted blessing that Catherine was? Hearing it made my stomach turn. I could only imagine the pain and horror she must have felt living it. I pushed back my distaste as Catherine continued:

"I wasn't strong enough to go against my father and Peter. Whenever I tried, my dad would have Peter lock me in one of the rooms he kept for clients. Sometimes they'd keep me in there for days with little food and water, really just enough to keep me going. Whenever I tried to run away, Peter would drag me back and dad would watch as he beat me. They never hit my face or anywhere too visible, they still needed me to look good when I performed in the main club. But they'd leave me weak and too tired to try again, at least for a little while."

I was horrified with what Catherine was saying. My stomach turning with every word and I had no clue how she wasn't constantly in tears, how she was even speaking about all this without crying. I did my best to keep my expressions to a minimum, not wanting her to stop. I silently prayed it wouldn't get worse but all the while having a sickening feeling it was going to.

"I never saw any of the money they made from me when I worked… in that way. Performing in the club happened less and less. Eventually I stopped altogether with the exception of special occasions and holidays. My father and Peter would keep a close eye on me whenever I was in public, making sure I behaved and didn't try anything. Though tolerable before, my life had become a living hell. Every day I wanted to run, but I had nowhere to go. I was a child, still in school, but I had no one to help me, no one to trust.

"I decided that once I graduated… once I was able to save up enough, I would find a way to leave and never look back. I figured anything would be better than the absolute hell I was living. So I saved. Every tip, every scrap of change I found, I pocketed. It wasn't much, but it got me one step closer to leaving.

"I graduated at eighteen and nine months later I was gone. I only had a couple of hundred in my pocket but I didn't care… it would have to be enough. I packed my bag with just a few clothes and my two favourite books, *The Princess Bride* and *Northanger Abbey*. I waited until they were asleep, then snuck out to catch the next bus out of town. And, just like that, I was free, free from the abuse and the pain. Finally free of the family I had grown to hate. Sadly, I was foolish and naive to think that this was true. It was just the desperate hope of a child.

"I didn't have a plan or anything when I left, where to go or what to do, so I stayed on the bus until I was a few towns away and made it to Belleville that first night. From there, I hit Kingston, then Prescott up to Ottawa. I found waitressing jobs in every place I stayed, and made enough cash to move on to the next town. Once I hit Ottawa, I found a club where I could sing. I still waitressed, after tips it paid better, but it was nice to sing again. Every day though I was so afraid my father or Peter would find me so I kept moving to different towns. Eventually, I left Ontario all together and slowly made my way across the country. I figured the further away I got, the less likely I would be found.

"Wherever I landed, I always kept to myself; I didn't want to risk bringing people into my life, paranoid I would be found. I figured if anyone came, it would be Peter. It broke my heart that my own brother would hurt me in so many ways but I knew he was just doing what our father ordered, wanting to please him."

As I listened, I tried to imagine the fear Catherine experienced, living every day never knowing if she was safe. I tightened my grip on her hand, my heart breaking as she spoke. I knew her story wasn't going to be pleasant but I never imagined all this. The truth is, her past only made me love her more, escaping an abusive home and family, travelling alone, takes a strength most people don't have. I was amazed.

"By the time I made it to Calgary, I was hoping to stay hidden in the city. After six months, I was considering calling Calgary my new home. I found a bachelor suite for reasonable rent and a job in a club as a server. I felt like I was finally putting my life together.

"One night when I was on shift, the regular singer called in. Her band had just nailed a tour across Canada and the US, they were leaving in the morning. She quit and management moved me up to be the main lounge singer, but that is when Peter found me."

"It was a complete fluke, he had no idea I worked there but had come into the club looking for a drink with his buddy Alec Wilford. I had no idea what they were doing in Calgary, what had brought them so far from home.

"The moment I saw them both I knew I was in trouble. The second my last song finished, I ran off the stage to the back room. I quickly grabbed my purse from the table and headed for the back exit. I prayed they didn't see me and that I could get away and not have to face them. I actually made it back to my place and started packing a bag when Peter and Alec barged in. I had never seen Peter angrier than at that moment. Alec closed and locked the door behind him and stood, arms crossed as he watched Peter yell:

"You little bitch! You fucking whore! You don't work for anyone but us, you don't sing for anyone but us. You belong to us and do as your fucking told."

"As he yelled I couldn't help the tears falling and I knew there was no one to save me. Peter's eyes were wide and fierce. With his fists clenched tightly and his knuckles turning white, he came at me. Beating me, Peter continued to yell:

"I'll teach you to fuck off, teach you to disobey," he screamed on and on until I passed out. I don't remember much after that. Apparently, one of my neighbours heard Peter yelling and called the police. Peter was arrested but Alec got away. He heard the sirens and bailed while Peter was still beating me."

"My God!" I couldn't hold my tongue any longer. Her own brother beating her, all because she started a new life. I was full of anger and disgust for her family treating her like this. No one deserves a life like that. I made a mental note to try to fix things with Thomas. We had problems sure, and we didn't always get along, but we'd never be so cruel, never purposely damage each other's lives. Catherine sat across from me. I instinctively wiped the small tear that fell from her wide eyes. "I'm sorry, I'm so sorry love," I whispered. I placed a light kiss on her cheek once her tear was gone, I silenced myself, letting her continue.

"Thanks," Catherine said a little hoarse, "Peter was charged with attempted murder and because he had a prior criminal record he was sentenced to prison. I was hospitalized. Peter had broken four of my ribs, ruptured my spleen, broken my collarbone and right arm, fractured my left leg, and caused a brain bleed. In short, I was badly beaten, concussed and suffering from the brain bleed. The doctors monitored me closely, for weeks I could scarcely open my eyes or respond to anyone. I woke up almost a month later. I remained in the hospital for about two and a half months before they would release me.

"The police had spoken to me, asking what happened with Peter, if I knew why he attacked me. I'm sure they already knew why, but they wanted it from me. That was the last time I saw Peter. When I got my strength back, I packed my bag and moved again."

"You came here?" I asked.

"I came here, met your aunts my first week and they took me in and, well you know the rest. Betty and Ronnie showed me what family really was. I know Peter went to prison but I have no idea if he's still in or not. Even with everything I endured, some things just never seemed to add up. I was in that hospital for months and not once did anyone else come for me. I knew my father would not have come for me himself, he hated to travel, and never liked being away from his business. I thought for sure he'd send someone else. Every day I spent stuck in that hospital I wondered if someone would show up. I wondered that is, until now."

"Wait. What do you mean until now?" I interrupted with concern.

"Alec Wilford, whom I mentioned earlier, Peter's friend, he's the man who's been coming to The Old Black Curtain.

"That big tattooed guy who's been showing up at the club? Seriously? Why didn't you tell me earlier? I would have… I would have done something." As I spoke, I regretted my quick response. She was scared and my fear for her safety was getting the best of me.

Catherine was trying desperately to hold back tears, "I… I don't know what to do. I like it here. I'm finally happy. I've built a home, I have friends, family, and you Michael — I have you. I don't… I don't want to lose you. And I'm terrified Alec is going to tell my father where I am, and…"

Catherine stopped fighting her tears, finally relieved to share her burden — she let everything out. She had been keeping so much to herself. Catherine looked tired, unsure of what to do. My heart broke for her, for the girl who had survived more than anyone ever should. I cradled her in my arms with her head on my chest. I stroked her hair and just let her cry. By the time she stopped crying, it was almost dawn.

"You changed everything, Michael. Everything," Catherine breathed as she dried her eyes.

"Change is good." I comforted her.

"No, you don't understand, uhm…" Catherine paused for a moment, trying to find the words to express what she meant. "Before you, there was only pain and shame. I felt tainted by my past and hated myself. Then you came into my life and it's like a light came on. You inspire me to be more, to be who I want to be and not what the past made me. You woke me up, Michael. You make me better." Catherine couldn't help the tears from falling again. She was completely open and vulnerable and all I could do was try not to cry myself. Her words meant more to me than she could know.

"You make me better too," I whispered before taking her in my arms again.

We were exhausted but neither of us could sleep. We lay curled up, wrapped around each other and I didn't dare let go. Catherine was quiet and safe in my arms. I planned to keep her that way. After a while, I told her what I thought we should do:

"Tomorrow we are going to the police."

"No!" Catherine sat up the moment I spoke.

"Cat, after everything you told me, and with Alec hanging around, I'm not taking any chances. I'm sorry, but we need to go to the police. You're not safe with him around and I'll be damned if I let anything happen to you."

"Michael, no, I'm not — we're not —"

"Give me one good reason not to?" I interrupted.

"It will get out... my life, my fucked up life and everyone will know. I just... I can't... I can't face that. I'm sorry, I can't." Catherine was practically shaking as she spoke. "Michael, I'm sorry for..." I stopped her, shaking my head and planting a gentle kiss on her forehead. Taking a hold of her again and wrapping my arms around her to settle her shaking form.

"No, no," I said, "You don't ever have to be sorry, after everything you've been through." I kissed her again. "You're safe with me, you don't have to worry about anything. I'm going to take care of everything from now on. No one will ever hurt you again. I promise."

Catherine didn't say anything, she simply leaned back into me as we settled comfortably in bed. I placed a kiss upon her head and held her tightly in my arms. Catherine drifted off to sleep as I ran all that new information through my mind. How does someone survive all that? How does someone even function? I knew she didn't want to bring the police in but, how could I keep her safe? Alec was out there watching her and God knows what he's up too. Has he told her family she's here? Are they coming for her?

The prospect of moving back to London was looking like a more and more appealing option, if only I could convince Catherine to join me. I still wasn't sure she'd come. She was attached to living on the island, and for the first time in her life, she had found stability and didn't want to lose it. Change was hard for everyone, I could only imagine it was twice as hard for Catherine. I decided to call Hamish in the morning, get his opinion on what to do about Alec. Of course, Hamish would likely feel the need to approach him and knock him out. But that was not a feasible option. I'd have to think of something else but I knew one thing for sure, Catherine was going to stay safe.

CHAPTER EIGHT

Lost Melody

THE RAVEN TATTOOED Alec Wilford seemed to have vanished. He stopped coming to The Old Black Curtain and Catherine worried he had gone back to her father. She started talking about packing up and leaving, moving on again to a new town before Alec or someone else came for her. I was doing my best to calm her, trying to put her anxiety at bay, but her fears were valid. With each passing day we didn't see Alec, the more paranoid she became.

For the first time Catherine was torn about what to do. She had never wanted to stay before, never had people worth staying for. Catherine's first instinct was to pack up and run but her love for the community, Zoey, The Old Black Curtain, all made her hesitate. Then there was me standing in her way, she had found someone to love without pain and fear. Catherine had finally created a life for herself; a good life and she didn't want to give it up.

I suggested we move to London. I would have to return sooner or later and now seemed as good a time as any. I felt it was a wise move and believed Catherine was tempted, but she was still unsure. She loved where she lived and wondered if running away was really the best option.

While Catherine was thinking it over, I received a text from Hamish. Apparently, the board was beginning to make waves regarding my prolonged absence. Rumours were starting to spin through the office that I was never coming back. Hamish had a bad feeling and suggested I come back for a week or so to save face. I didn't want to think about M&M Tech, or the issues my Board of Directors were having. I could only think about Catherine. It seemed, however, the more I tried to ignore the problems back home, the worse things appeared to get. Catherine wasn't ready to leave Victoria yet, and I knew better than to pressure her. Hamish was at least sympathetic to my plight, he understood why I wanted to stay. He texted constantly asking about Zoey. He was determined, after our business affairs settled down, to find a way to be with her.

All the talk of returning to London put Thomas in the forefront of my mind. It had been months since we'd spoken. Our last words to each other were in anger regarding Catherine. I wondered if perhaps it was time to reconcile things with him, for both of us to start behaving like brothers. The thought of leaving Catherine alone, if only for a week, without being sure where Alec was, made me extremely anxious. The idea of something happening to Catherine while I was away kept me up at night.

Eventually, Catherine convinced me to fly home, to help Hamish with the Board, and smooth things over with Thomas. She assured me she'd be okay for a week, we would figure out what to do about Alec when I returned. So I booked my flight and prepared for my trip, while spending every free moment with Catherine. The night before my flight Catherine and I sat at our usual table at The Old Black Curtain. Wanting to make the night special, I had a gift for her, a fourteen-carat white gold necklace with a musical note pendant. I had been waiting for the right moment to give it to her as a memento of all we shared. The necklace was just the first step. I had high hopes of one day giving Catherine the perfect ring and asking her to be my wife. I knew Catherine was not ready for that move yet, heck, I was just coming out of a divorce myself. But I would wait, for as long as she needed.

After we had finished our first round of drinks, Catherine left to get ready for her set. Raymond brought my second round to the table and soon Catherine was on stage singing her rendition of Nat King Cole's 'The Autumn Leaves.' Sipping on my whiskey and entranced by Catherine's voice, I felt calm and content. Her next song began and my heart hung on every single word:

> *I have a melody to sing*
> *That I don't know how to play*
> *The words are locked inside of me*
> *Struggling to be free*
> *So I'll keep on searching*
> *For the tears I can't show*
> *I'll keep singing*
> *For the words I can't say*

*I'm lost in a haze
That's clouding my light
Though I've been led astray
I know I'll be alright*

*And I'll stay strong
Not let the world take me
I'll find my lost word
My lost melodies*

*So I'll keep on searching
For the tears I can't show
I'll keep singing
For the words I can't say
I'll keep on fighting
Till my last day
I'll keep screaming
Till I am heard*

*Oh I have a melody to sing
But I don't know how to play'*

Catherine singing another original was breathtaking, we never lost eye contact the entire time. Honestly, if I wasn't already head over heels in love with her, I would have fallen all over again right then and there. Hearing Catherine sing, especially with such confidence, always put me at ease. No matter what was happening in our lives, no matter what chaos was surrounding us, her voice always centered me. After a few more jazz standards, Catherine came back to our table and Raymond brought the third round of drinks.

I had to remind myself to breathe, it was our last night together and I wanted to remember every part of it and every inch of her. I was dreading leaving, spending time away from Catherine would be torture, and with Alec mysteriously disappearing, it made me nervous. Leaving Catherine without any protection terrified me more than I wanted to admit. All I wanted was for her to be safe by my side, always. Catherine noticed the worried expression on my face.

"Everything alright?" she asked, concern flooding her voice.

"Oh yes, love, just a lot on my mind is all." I did my best to look calm and said, "That was beautiful as always, Cat." She blushed as I complimented her.

"Thank you, Michael." She said, taking a sip of her drink and trying to hide her blushing face. She never could accept a compliment.

I reached for the small black jewellery box in my inner coat pocket and gently placed it in front of Catherine as she set down her drink. Surprise and confusion emerged on her pretty face as she quietly stared at the little black box. She took a deep breath before picking up the box and opening it. A huge, happy smile lit up her face, along with a slight sigh of relief. Poor girl must have thought I was proposing, but I knew she wasn't ready yet.

She took the necklace out of the box and clasped it around her neck. "It's beautiful, Michael, thank you, I love it." Catherine leaned over and softly kissed my cheek.

Catherine came with me to the airport, wanting to see me off. I kissed her goodbye, promising I'd be back before she knew it and made my way through security. Waiting for the plane to board, Hamish rang. I figured he was calling to make sure I was actually on my way.

"Hamish, I'm just waiting for the plane. I should be there as scheduled."

"Ahh, that's good, mucker, 'cause we have a serious problem."

"What kind of problem?"

"The Board's convened a meetin'— they're talkin' about firin' ya cause you're ne'er here no more."

"Fire me! They can't fire me Hamish. This is my company, our comp — we built M&M Tech together and they cannot just fire me. Do they even have the shares? The votes?" My head was spinning with the likelihood of being fired from my own company.

"I dunnae mucker, but we'd better fin' out," Hamish said. "But mind, I'm on your side here."

"I'm sorry, Hamish, I know. And I appreciate you keeping the Board at bay as long as you have. Ah, look they're calling my flight number, I gotta go. I'll see you when I land."

"I'll be there," Hamish confirmed before we hung up.

I boarded my plane with more worries: M&M Tech, Hamish's stress level, my brother Thomas, and Catherine, always Catherine. With everything happening, I tried to stay focused and think about what to say to the Board, what I could do to help Hamish. My thoughts kept straying back to Catherine. I had a nagging feeling that leaving her was the wrong move. I tried to shake it off but my life back in London was beginning to try my patience. I felt split in two; one-half longing to stay by Catherine's side while the other was determined to save my life's work.

My hope was to be in London for as short a time as possible. I would convince the Board I was fully committed to my company, and try to rectify things with Thomas, if possible. If everything went my way, I figured I'd be back in Catherine's arms within a week. I met Hamish at the arrivals gate with my carry on and we headed straight to the office. As Hamish drove, I could tell he was on edge. A rarity for him, but with the board pressuring him, he was bound to be put out.

My corner office was just as I had left it so many months before. I had forgotten how much I loved the view. I walked behind my desk and stared out the large bay windows. Looking out I saw Big Ben and took a deep breath to try to relieve the chaos in my head. I looked around my large empty office, wondering how I had spent so many hours there instead of being out in the world, living life. My desk was practically empty, nothing on it but the computer monitor, mouse, keyboard, and my phone. There wasn't even a pen sitting atop. I had no photos, nothing personal of any kind as it had never occurred to me to put out any of my life's mementos around me. When I was working, that's all I did, completely focused on the task at hand. The walls were a drab grey-sliver with some art hanging that I had never bothered to look at. A built-in bookcase on the left wall was filled with nothing but business texts, and to the right there was a small seating area for meetings. There was a beige loveseat and matching armchairs with a glass coffee table in the middle. Behind the seating area was an ensuite bathroom.

Hamish had left me in my office, I had just under an hour before the meeting with the Board at four o'clock. I texted Thomas to let him know I was back in town. He replied saying he'd be home all night and to come round when I was done at the office. Tossing my phone next to my bag, I went to freshen up and change into the one decent suit I had with me while my mind was occupied with ever-racing thoughts.

At four o'clock, Hamish and I made our way to the conference room where the eight Board members sat waiting. We closed the door and barely sat down when Mr. Graft started speaking.

"Mr. Murphy, let me be blunt. You need to return to work or you will be removed from this company. This has gone on long enough."

"First, I never left. I have been in full contact with Hamish the entire time I've been in Canada. Second, I don't believe there is any clause stating I cannot run my end of things away from the office, and third, most importantly, this is my company. Hamish and I built this place out of nothing, hired each and every one of you. So don't think for a second you can oust me." My tone was harsher than I intended but I wanted to pay Mr. Graft the respect of being as blunt as he had been with me.

"Mr. Murphy, we have the votes. We can and will remove you if you don't agree to relocate back here." Mr. Graft was speaking for the whole Board, everyone nodded in agreement while Hamish and I sat in disbelief of their boldness.

"No, if Michael goes, so do I. You cannot fire him," Hamish chimed in my defence. I looked at Hamish with shock. We never discussed him quitting if I got the boot.

"We'll leave an' start anew if you aren't careful." Hamish nodded at me, he had clearly thought this through.

"Mr. MacPhail, let's not be rash here. There's no reason for anyone to leave if Mr. Murphy simply agrees to move back and continue his duties as CEO." Mr. Graft was trying to backtrack, he hadn't expected Hamish to threaten to leave if they were successful in firing me.

"I need to be in Canada right now." I said, "What if I take an extended sabbatical?"

"You've already taken too many months of leave. This business is moving forward, stocks on M&M Tech are on the rise. You and Hamish are the face of this company, not being here and running things is proving to be problematic for the business. So, either agree to come back full time or we will remove you. As I said, we have the votes."

"You may have the votes but not the capital. Hamish and I still hold the majority share. You can't afford to axe me from the company," I said. I was hoping the mention of money would put an end to it.

"That's not entirely true. We can buy you out, Mr. Murphy," Mr. Graft said and passed a manila folder across the table to me. "Here's our offer. Take it and go, or return to work."

"What makes you think I will take your offer?"

"Let's be honest, Mr. Murphy, you are not here anymore and you haven't been for quite some time. We understand that death changes people and no one blames you for your absence. Nevertheless, it is time to make a decision before this company is affected negatively, so either come back and run this company like you are supposed to or let us buy you out. That is our offer, I think you will find it reasonable. We'll give you some time to think everything over, but not too much time."

As Mr. Graft finished I opened the folder to read their offer. I looked over at Hamish before passing it to him. Mr. Graft and the rest of the board left the conference room to give us privacy to mull over their demand.

"Wow! That's quite the sum," Hamish said after everyone had left.

"Yeah … You go if I go? Really Hamish? You love this company. You can't leave if I get ousted."

"It's just a buildin', Michael — our company, our work, that's us. It's wherever we go and whatever we decide to do. Stuff them!" Hamish passed me the file back.

"Okay, so what do we do, then? Are they right? Am I done here?" I asked, sincerely wanting his opinion.

"Well, I'm biased. Ah want you here. So if you want to stay, we'll fin' a way. But you gotta ask yourself, do you feel done here?" Hamish said.

"I don't know Hamish. I just don't know. I mean, this is our life's work. I can't just walk away from it all."

"I think ya have your answer then." Hamish smiled. "You go, I go remember."

"You're a good man, Hamish." We both sat for a moment in the quiet conference room. I looked at the twenty-million offer the Board handed me. I could hardly believe that our little company was now worth so much and that's when I made my decision.

"Let's open offices in Victoria," I told Hamish.

"Really?"

"Really. Think about it, look at this offer. If they can afford to buy me out, we can afford to open offices in Victoria. It's where we both want to be anyway. It's where our hearts are."

"It's where the girls are, ya mean," Hamish said chuckling.

"You're telling me you don't want to be with Zoey?"

"Naw, I'm, gonna marry tha' one."

"And I'm going to marry Catherine."

"Sounds like a plan to me mucker."

"It does indeed." I took the Board's offer and tore it to pieces.

Hamish and I walked out of the conference room with resolve. We had a plan and we were not about to be bullied by our own Board of Directors. Hamish went back to his office. I checked the time, not realizing how late in the day it was. It was time to go and see Thomas. His flat was within walking distance from my office, so I grabbed my bag and headed out on foot. The last time I had walked these same streets was before Catherine had come into my life. So much had changed in the last few months. I had only been away for a day and already missed her.

As I slowly walked along, the brisk air filled my lungs and I breathed in deeply, preparing myself mentally to deal with Thomas. I checked the time, it was midnight in London, and roughly four in the afternoon in Victoria. Catherine would still be at the bookstore. I decided to call, check-in, and wish her a good day. Her phone was ringing. Catherine normally picked up on the second or third ring, but by the eighth I hung up, confused and worried. Catherine always answered the phone. I racked my mind for the reason she missed the call: Did she close early? Was she already at The Old Black Curtain on stage or in the back getting ready? Was she out with Zoey? No, she would have picked up even if she was with Zoey.

I arrived at Thomas's flat and went in, my mind still on where Catherine might be. I poured myself a generous glass of scotch and as I took a sip, I heard shuffling steps coming down the hallway. I turned to see Thomas; I must have woken him.

"Oh Michael, you're back," he said, in a sleepy voice. "You sort everything out yet?" I thought it odd that Thomas had been asleep, the man loved the nightlife of London. I couldn't shake the feeling that something was wrong.

"No, not yet. The board gave me an ultimatum, actually. Relocate back to London or let them buy me out." I turned back to Thomas's bar to pour him a drink. I offered it to him as I waited for his response.

"So just move back," Thomas said before taking the glass from me, then taking a generous sip.

"I have a life in Victoria." I said, shaking my head, "I have Catherine, Zoey, friends. I'm happy there."

"Sorry, Michael, I don't know what to tell you, but it doesn't look like you can have both. It comes down to your girlfriend or your company." Thomas finished off his drink then poured himself another. "But for the record," he said, "you're an idiot if you choose that girl over your company."

"It is not that simple. Not that black and white." I could already feel him start to get under my skin. Once again, Thomas continued to be an insensitive ass, but I tried to keep myself in check as we spoke. "Besides, Hamish and I came up with a plan and the Board will have no choice but to accept it."

"Michael, seriously, you are going to fight the Board? Are you really going to throw your life's work away all for the sake of one overpaid librarian? What has that girl done to you? I don't even recognize you anymore." Thomas said as he paced the length of his living room.

"Good," I said. "I'm glad I seem different to you. 'That girl', as you call her, has changed me, made me a better man. And I'm not fighting the board, Hamish and I decided to open offices in Victoria. We'll hire a chief of operations to run the London office, just like we did for the Scotland office, and expand into Canada." I downed the rest of my drink and poured another.

My drink refilled, I turned to face Thomas, bracing myself for his reaction. We'd had arguments and differences of opinions before, where I had certainly lost my temper, as has he, but I was supposed to be the level headed one. Thomas was always the wild and impulsive one, but things were different now, I was different. I was stronger, more confident, and I didn't have to put up with my brother's snide remarks about my personal life. As I came to these realizations, a small smirk started to grow across Thomas's face. I took another large sip of whisky before asking him:

"Find all this amusing do you?"

"Yes, actually I do," he responded, "I always knew you had it in you. Good to see you stop being so damn polite and proper for a change. She's really done a number on you, hasn't she? Shame, really."

As Thomas spoke, my phone started to buzz. I pulled it out of my pocket, hoping it was Catherine getting back to me. I didn't recognize the number but the message was clear. A photo of Catherine, beaten, holding up a newspaper with today's date. The caption simply stated:

"She's yours for $100,000."

CHAPTER NINE

Waiting Game

"HELLO? EARTH TO Michael?" Thomas was trying to get my attention as I continued to stare at my phone. It took me a few minutes before I even realized Thomas was speaking.

"Sorry. What?" I eventually asked.

"What's so fascinating on your phone? Catherine send you a dirty picture or something?" Thomas asked sarcastically, unaware of what was going on.

"No." I said quietly, still trying to process what had happened through my shock. "She's been kidnapped. It's a ransom text." I passed my phone over to Thomas.

"Shit." He said as he viewed the image and the demand beneath it. I downed the rest of my scotch before Thomas could hand me back my phone.

"Hundred thousand dollars. Bold. Whoever has her is smart. They know you have money and how much of a sap you are for her. Figured you'd pay just about anything to get her back," Thomas said as he as took another sip of his scotch. I stood there, suddenly anger replacing my shock faster than I expected.

"A sap? Her life is on the line and you're standing there mocking me?"

"Take a breath, have another drink. Look on the bright side, you and Hamish don't need to open offices in Victoria anymore. I mean, with Catherine gone you have no reason to go back." Thomas took a seat and continued drinking. My whole world was ending and all he could see was the business side of things.

"She's not gone, Thomas, she's been taken. She's been taken but can be saved. Think like a lawyer for crying out loud."

"Like a lawyer, fine. Look, when you or the police catch whoever took her, I will happily represent your girlfriend and get her all sorts of settlement. But the likelihood of saving her is slim to none, so why bother?"

"I just need to pay the ransom and I'll get her back. That's how these things work." I was pacing the room as I spoke, unable to stand still even for a moment.

Thomas was up out of his chair yelling: "PAY! You can't pay Michael. It's one-hundred-thousand dollars. They probably won't even release her, just take the money and run. Or, what's to stop them from just demanding more and more? Besides, no one is worth that kind of money."

"SHE IS!" I bellowed back at him.

The anguish and anger in my voice caused Thomas to take a step back. He could see the rage in my features and knew I was not going to back down.

"Michael," he said softly.

"No, no, Thomas. For once in your life, try thinking of someone other than yourself. I love her. If I can save her by giving up one-hundred-thousand dollars to get her back, then goddammit, that is exactly what I'm going to do."

My breathing was quick and shallow as I continued to pace. I tried to calm myself, to push back my rage and anger, to keep a clear logical head. Thomas took another sip of his drink before responding to me.

"You are throwing everything away," he said calmly, "all for the sake of one girl. Let her go. Start over."

He put his glass down on the table beside his chair as I took in what he said. I stood there with my hand tightening around my glass, tension setting my jaw, shaking my head slowly and deliberately. He didn't get it. He didn't understand that Catherine was now my everything. My soul was broken without her. I wanted to scream, and shout, but none of that would help. Standing there in my outrage, I lost all sense of reason.

I'd finally had enough. I threw my glass behind me and lunged forward, tackling Thomas to the ground. He had no time to react before I laid my fists into him. Thomas cried out as I continued my assault. He tried to defend himself, blocking a few of my strikes while I managed to land others. I knew I should stop, that hurting him wouldn't accomplish anything. None of this was even his fault, but now I was running on autopilot, beyond sensibility. I should have been no match for Thomas — he should have overpowered me. But my fury and passion gave me the force I needed to keep him down. I blamed myself for what had happened to Catherine, but Thomas's complete lack of empathy and understanding made him a convenient scapegoat for the moment. A place to relieve my own horrible sense of guilt. So I kept laying into my brother, until all my strength was gone.

We both lay still on the floor, catching our breath. Thomas, flat on his back, was taking slow, deep breaths, as his face started to become puffy and purple from my attack. I was a few inches from him, leaning against the couch, watching his chest rise and fall with every breath he took. I hadn't done any serious damage to him, he'd be bruised for a few weeks and might have a broken rib or two, but nothing life-threatening. Once I'd caught my own breath I pushed myself off the floor, stepped around him, and walked into the kitchen. I grabbed a cloth from the rack next to the fridge and dampened it with cold water from the sink. I went back to Thomas, who hadn't moved from his spot, and handed him the cold cloth. Thomas reached his hand out, taking the cloth from me, and laid it on his face for a brief moment before starting to clear the blood away. After cleaning himself up a little, Thomas finally shifted enough to sit up, leaning against the chair. As he moved, he gave a slight wince of pain and clutched at his side.

"I think you may have broken something," Thomas spat out.

"Sorry. I... I just feel so lost," I said as calmly as I could muster. I knew I shouldn't have taken my anger and frustration out on him, but he'd pushed me over the edge.

"She's just a girl, Michael. There are thousands of them out there. Come home, find another one and start again. Get things back to normal."

"I can't. I can't walk away from her. She is my normal."

We sat in silence as I tried to determine how to fix the mess my life had become. Finding Catherine and getting her back became my top priority. I hated myself at that moment. Berated myself for leaving her in the first place, I should have ignored the Board's demands and stayed in Victoria to look out for Catherine. It was only a job after all, just a company. I could always find work, or what the hell, not work at all at this stage of my life. I walked out of the living room leaving Thomas on the floor. I grabbed my bag, checking to see that my passport was still in the outside pocket, and went back to Thomas.

"I'm leaving. I know you don't understand but I have to get her back. I just have to." I paused for a moment, letting my words sink in. Thomas slowly rose from the floor, holding onto his right side.

"I'm sorry for… for everything." I hoped Thomas would accept my apology, knowing I didn't really deserve it. I had crossed the line and I knew it.

"Do what you need to do then, Michael. I don't get it, or get her, but I clearly can't stop you. So that's the end of it, then." Thomas turned and walked away from me.

Things with Thomas had not gone well at all. We didn't repair a single thing. In fact, I was pretty sure I had made things worse. But, my brother, and our relationship would have to wait for another day, another time. I realized that not everything can be fixed, and sometimes you have to just let things be. I left my brother's flat with the hope that someday things would be different between us. Until then,

I needed to focus on my current predicament — how to get Catherine back.

I hailed a taxi and went to Hamish's place. I knew, no matter what, he would help me. Hamish was still up when I got there. With a drink in hand, he welcomed me in. I showed him the image of Catherine and the ransom demand. I filled Hamish in on who I thought might have abducted her. The first person who came to mind was Alec. After everything Catherine had told me about him, I wouldn't put it past him to take her. I explained Catherine's history with Alec and Hamish agreed, it seemed logical that Alec was the most likely suspect. I told him that our plans for the Board would have to wait. I was catching the next flight to Victoria.

"Stuff the Board. Is Zoey alright?" Hamish put down his drink then pulled out his phone and dialed Zoey's number. I waited in anticipation, praying that at least Zoey was all right, but after a couple of minutes Hamish hung up the phone.

"No answer. I'm coming too," he said and headed out of the room to quickly pack a bag. At that moment, I couldn't have been prouder to be Hamish's friend. The fact that he would drop everything, the Board and the day-to-day work in our company all for the sake of Catherine and Zoey, was mind-blowing.

When we first met and became friends, Hamish had a new girl every week, then every month. Since Zoey, he'd completely changed, her well-being took priority. It was good to see my friend happily settling down. I truly hoped Zoey was ok.

As Hamish packed I called the airport looking for two first-class tickets for the next available flight to Victoria. We lucked out — a flight was leaving at six in the morning with only one stop at Sea-Tac airport in Washington State, giving us plenty of time to get there. This was turning into one of my longest nights ever. No sleep, an early flight and no idea what Hamish and I would be walking into. On top of that, I hadn't heard anything new from Catherine's kidnapper. Time felt frozen. Everything was taking forever and all I wanted was to have Catherine back in my arms, but I was beginning to worry that I never would.

The drive to the airport, checking in — Hamish handled almost everything. Once we were on the plane I told Hamish about my fight with Thomas, and he couldn't help but laugh. He said he wished he could have been there to see it. Hamish and I passed the long flight the best we could, trying not to think the worst and come up with a plan. We knew Catherine was gone but we had no idea if Zoey was okay. Hamish's mind was focused on her, hoping she was safe and unharmed. While of course, I hoped for the same thing, I couldn't stop thinking about Catherine. I prayed that wherever she was, she wasn't being harmed further. The only solace was believing she knew that I would come for her, that I would do anything, no matter what.

When we landed, we took a cab to the bookshop first. Hamish wanted to get to Zoey but we both needed to freshen up. The street was dark and empty. I quickly unlocked the shop door and headed in. Everything looked in order, which told me she hadn't been taken from here. I didn't bother turning on any of the lights as we made our way up to the apartment. We dropped our bags off to the side of the entrance and sighed in exhaustion.

"Why don't you freshen up? I'm gonna check on Zoey. I cannot wait." Hamish said. I nodded to him, then he headed back downstairs and out of the shop. I knew Zoey would be in good hands, once Hamish got to her. I flicked a light on, loosened my tie and headed for the shower.

After twenty-four hours without sleep, I grabbed a fresh set of clothes and dressed. I checked my phone before heading over to Zoey's place. Hamish had left me a message. Zoey was in the hospital. He texted her room number and told me to get there quick. I called a cab and twenty minutes later I was by his side, shocked. Whoever had taken Catherine had beaten Zoey and left her for dead. She and Catherine had been at home when the abduction took place. A nurse filled Hamish in on how Zoey was found. A neighbour walking their dog noticed their front door wide open and went to check it out, to see if everything was all right. Zoey was lying unconscious on the kitchen floor and Catherine was nowhere in sight. The neighbour immediately called for an ambulance.

Zoey had listed Catherine as her emergency contact, but of course, the hospital staff didn't get a response when they called. Hamish explained to the young nurse that he was Zoey's other half and that Catherine, her roommate, was missing. The nurse offered him her sympathies and let him know the police would be coming to talk with him. Grateful to Hamish for filling me in, I silently swore to myself for not going to Zoey's first. As much as I wanted to be out looking for Catherine, I hadn't heard from the kidnapper since the first demand and didn't know where to go next. I had little to go on, so I sat with Hamish at Zoey's bedside, praying she would wake soon.

An hour later, I left Hamish's to grab us both some coffee. When I returned Hamish was standing beside Zoey's bed speaking to a detective. He was a tall, thin man in dark jeans and a grey button down collared shirt. He had short, dark, brownish-black hair, full-rimmed glasses and a well-trimmed goatee.

"Michael," Hamish interrupted the detective to acknowledge me, "This is Detective John Oscar. He's here about Zoey." I shook the detective's hand, after handing Hamish his coffee.

"What do you know so far, detective?" I asked. I looked over Zoey's unconscious form before turning back to the detective.

"Well, I was hoping you both might be able to shed some light on the matter, actually. How do you know Ms. Johnson?" Oscar inquired.

"She's my better half," Hamish said quietly while taking Zoey's hand in his own.

"I see, and you Mr. ...?" Oscar asked, looking in my direction.

"Murphy. Michael Murphy," I answered, "I'm dating her best friend, Catherine. We're all like family, really."

"Catherine Miller?" Oscar said, looking at his notebook, "The roommate. Do either of you know where Ms. Miller is? No one can seem to contact her."

Hamish and I shared a momentary glace trying to decide what to do. Do we tell him what we know? By law, we were bound to. The idea of keeping Catherine's kidnapping to ourselves crossed my mind — to just keep things simple, pay them and get her back. But I knew it would never work like that. Look at what they had done to Zoey, who knew what they would do to Catherine, whether I paid them or not. The police would help keep her safe and provide a wider search net. Hamish nodded his head ever so slightly and I knew we were on the same page. I pulled my phone out from my back pocket and pulled up the message, handing it over to Detective Oscar.

"I received this while in London. Hamish and I got on the first flight back. We found out that Zoey was here in the hospital and we're still waiting on instructions concerning Catherine." I took a breath to calm myself. Talking about Catherine and her abduction made my mind race and heart pound.

"A hundred thousand dollars. You have that kind of money?" Oscar asked.

"Yes," "I don't care what it costs me, I just want her back," I said, trying to keep my emotions in check.

"Well, we ran a search on Ms. Miller when we couldn't contact her. She's not in our database or any other for that matter. No driver's licence, no social security number, no credit, nothing. Tell me, how well do you two know this girl?" Oscar inquired.

"What? No, that's — that's not... What do you mean she has no records?" I stammered.

"I mean your girl here doesn't exist. So how well do you know her? Is it possible she's not really missing? That's she's just after your money?" Detective Oscar was asking questions

I didn't want to think about. I could hear Thomas's voice in my head, laughing at the thought of Catherine swindling me. But I knew her, she would never do this. I could feel it in my gut, she was in danger and needed saving.

"I know her better than most." I said confidently, "No, this isn't Catherine. She isn't capable of hurting anyone. Someone has her. I don't care what your system says or doesn't say. She needs our help." I had to fight to keep myself from getting overly emotional.

"All right, Mr. Murphy. You know her best, so for now I will take your word. I am going to need you to come down to the station though. We will put a trace on your phone and when the next message comes in hopefully we will be able to locate them." Oscar kept my phone. It had officially become evidence and I was in for a rather long stay at the local police station. I wanted to stay with Hamish, with Zoey, in case she woke up, but I knew Hamish would tell me if that happened. I looked to Hamish sitting by Zoey's bedside, holding her hand in his and knew they'd be all right. I put my coat on and followed Oscar out, leaving Zoey to Hamish's care. All I could do now was wish for this whole ordeal to be over. I just wanted Zoey to wake, and Catherine's captor to reach out. I wanted to hold her in my arms once more. Instead, I felt as if the world had stopped spinning and I was trapped in an endless void of waiting.

At the station, the detectives around me were kind. They offered me bad coffee while Oscar and I sat waiting for the next message to come through. We must have sat there for almost two hours making idle small talk. He wasn't as dull as I had first thought. We discussed the case, Oscar wondering if I had any idea who would have taken Catherine. I told him about Alec Wilford, his relationship to Catherine and why she was scared of him. I explained how I had wanted to go to the police but Catherine had talked me out of it. I hated myself for that. Oscar ran Wilford's name through his database and sure enough, he showed up with quite the rap sheet. Alec Wilford, age 33, born in Kingston Ontario. Wilford was known for aggravated assault, theft, extortion, racketeering, drug possession and trafficking, the list went on and on. He was given an eight-year sentence but was out on parole after only three for good behaviour. After his release, he went to work for a Ralph Eden, owner of Eden's Bliss, a club in Toronto. It seemed to be a front for a brothel that was raided eight months ago. I tried to think back to when Alec first appeared at The Old Black Curtain. After Eden's Bliss was raided and shut down, it seems that's when he went searching for Catherine.

After a while, we moved on to more trivial small talk. About half way through our discussion of local soccer teams my phone vibrated, shaking the desk slightly. We both fell silent as Oscar picked up the phone, then read the message out loud. The captor wanted the one-hundred-thousand dollars in cash at eight o'clock tomorrow night, at what the detectives determined was an abandoned warehouse in Vancouver. My heart sank learning Catherine was no longer in Victoria. The knowledge that she was even farther away than I thought, somehow added much more weight to my pain and sense of loss. The wait to reach her, and the distance between us felt unbearable.

The time during Catherine's kidnapping was some of the worst of my life. Every minute felt like an hour, a day felt like a week, and each second that passed my heart grew weaker. The fear in my mind was louder than any other thoughts. I found myself dealing with things I had only seen in movies or read in books. When a news report would talk about another murder or abduction that had taken place, I always felt so bad for the victims and sympathetic for the families, but never truly understanding the impact of having someone taken from you must have felt like. But experiencing it, having your heart and soul ripped from you, is truly paralyzing. Each breath you take is laced with fear and doubt. Anxiety rises to levels you never thought possible and all you can do is try not to cry, to scream. All you can do is wait.

After I received the captor's instructions, things moved quickly. I phoned my accountant and arranged for the cash to be available and ready by the time Detective Oscar and I arrived at the bank. Oscar was sympathetic, but still held some doubts concerning Catherine's involvement in all of it. I did my best to ignore his trepidations. After the banking arrangement was done, I called Hamish to check-in. Sadly, Zoey was still unconscious and Hamish was going crazy. I filled him in about the exchange that was to happen in Vancouver. I reassured him that Zoey would wake and be fine. I'd come back with Catherine and we could put all this behind us. Hamish wished me luck. I knew he couldn't come along to help me out this time, he was needed where he was. While his duty was to Zoey, mine was to Catherine; I was going to bring her home.

Oscar ran through everything and assured me I would be one-hundred percent safe. They would have me wired up to hear what was going on and have eyes on me the whole time. The Vancouver RCMP would be discreetly positioned all around the warehouse assisting Detective Oscar in getting Catherine back safely. So, Oscar, two uniformed cops, and I caught the three p.m. ferry to Vancouver, giving us plenty of time to get to the station to prepare for my eight o'clock meeting.

At eight o'clock on the dot, I was standing in an abandoned warehouse with several police tuned in and one-hundred-thousand dollars stuffed into a large grey duffle bag. From what little I could see, the warehouse used to be an old mechanics garage. Auto parts were lying about the floor and a faded decal of a vintage yellow mustang was peeling from the front of what looked like an office. I checked my watch again, 8:12 pm, and still no sign of Catherine or her captor. Whoever had her was late and my anxiety and concern were in full bloom. I could hear Oscar in my ear telling me to stop fidgeting and remain calm, they'd be here soon.

I stood in that empty warehouse for over twenty minutes before a black SUV finally pulled in. The second the man got out of the car, I wanted to throttle him. Of course it was Alec Wilford.

"It's Alec. I'm not even surprised, he's been stalking her for weeks," I murmured through the wire. I rolled my one hand into a fist to restrain my rage. Remembering I needed to stay calm, I took a deep breath.

"Let me guess," I called out to him, "her family hired you to bring her back?"

"Not exactly, Murphy. No."

"Then why? Why take her? What good does it do?"

"It puts money in my pocket. I was left with nothing after the club got raided and they were arrested. I finally found her and she's with you, Mr. Moneybags, so pathetically in love with her. Sure to pay any price. Ha! You have no idea how much of a chump you are. But hey, it works out in my favour. Now, do you have the money?" Alec demanded.

"You're despicable!" I said, feeling sick to my stomach. I had to ignore it. All that mattered was getting Catherine away from him. "Yes, it's right here." I shifted the large heavy duffle bag at my feet to bring notice to it. "Where is she?" I asked again.

"All of it? It's all there?" Alec asked, not taking his eyes off the bag.

"Yes, it's all here, now please, just — where is she?" I was losing what little patience I had left and Alec was stalling, but I wasn't sure exactly why.

"God, you're like a broken record with this girl. Did it ever occur to you that you're better off without her? Hmm? Seriously, I've done you a favour. I mean, you don't even know her." Alec smirked as he spoke, I could tell he was trying to aggravate me. It was working, but I wasn't about to let him know that.

"I know Catherine. I love her."

"Oh, you poor, poor bastard. I'm telling you, you don't know her."

"And I suppose you do?"

"Yes, as a matter of fact. But whatever, if you want to throw away all your money for her, I'm not gonna complain.

Now give me the money and we can all go our separate ways." Alec reached his hand out in want of the duffle bag.

"No, bring Catherine out. Let me see she's okay then the money's all yours.

"No. Money first."

Looking at Alec, we were officially at an impasse. I wasn't giving him the money without seeing Catherine and he wasn't giving her up without the money. The more I watched him, the more I sensed something was wrong. He was looking all over the place, unable to stand still, one foot constantly pointed back at his SUV. That's when it dawned on me.

"You don't have her, do you?" My voice stern, I could hear Oscar in my ear telling me to stay calm and to not spook Alec. He wanted me to get him to confirm she wasn't here, then they'd take him.

"Of course I have her. Now give me the money," Alec shouted, yelling at me now with rage and fury.

"You are out of your mind if you think I'm giving you a hundred-thousand dollars without Catherine in return. Now where is she?" I yelled right back at him.

"Gone… OK… Dammit," Alec said in defeat. We could hear the sirens in the background and time was running out.

"Gone? What? What do you mean gone?" I stammered in disbelief.

"Seriou—" Alec started in, but I cut him off.

"Did you even have her at all? Why bother to do any of this if you don't have her?" I could hear Oscar in my ear telling me this was done, they would be there in a few seconds and we'd find Catherine some other way. I ignored the detective and stared at Alec, waiting for an answer.

"Yes, okay, I took her, and when I sent you the ransom demand I did have her but she got away."

"YOU LOST HER?" I yelled. We could hear the sirens loud and clear now, they were right outside the warehouse and time had run out. Alec kept shifting his gaze between the bag and me. He looked like he was gonna try and run for it and was deciding if he could take my money on his way out. We both looked towards the large bay door where the police were coming in. At that moment, Alec bolted straight towards me. He knocked me to the ground before being caught at the door behind me. They pinned him to the ground and cuffed his hand behind his back. I got up and took a few steps towards him before Oscar put a hand on my arm to keep me back.

"You're gonna look for her, aren't you?" Alec asked me once they got him up.

"Yes," was all I said.

"You shouldn't, I'm telling you. Let her go. You don't know her. You don't even know her name," Alec said as Oscar took over his custody leading him out to the squad car.

I stood there in shock and denial. It took me a minute to find my bearings and really take in what Alec had said. I needed answers and my ticket to them was almost gone. Soon Alec would be unreachable. The police would lock him down and I'd never speak to him again. Seeing that the detective and Alec were nearly at the car, I ran to catch up to them.

"What do you mean? What do you mean I don't know her name? Alec? What do you mean?" But I was too late. I was yelling at him as Oscar closed the car door. Alec just looked at me through the thick bullet-proof glass window, a slow, malicious smile spreading across his face.

CHAPTER TEN

Catherine

I NEVER GAVE up hope that I'd find Catherine, but as much as Detective Oscar kept me in the loop regarding the investigation, I still had more questions than answers. After the Vancouver fiasco, I returned to the Victoria General Hospital to check on Hamish and Zoey. Detective Oscar said it would be a while before he would have any news on Catherine. So I waited with Hamish at the hospital for news, for Zoey to wake. I honestly wasn't sure how Hamish managed it; he was relentless, never leaving Zoey's side on the off chance she'd wake. The doctors told us she was in a minimally conscious state and she could wake up at any time now. They had repaired the brain bleed and saw no further damage. It was up to Zoey now. Hamish and I sat, day after day, waiting. I would get him food and supply him with coffee determined to keep him healthy as we prayed for Zoey's recovery.

It was four more days before Zoey woke. Unfortunately, for Hamish, she woke up about five minutes after I had finally convinced him to take a walk and get some air. The only way to get him to take a break was to promise not to leave Zoey's side. When I saw Zoey open her eyes, I called for a doctor and Hamish appeared a second later, he must have only been walking the hallway refusing to venture too far from her. I hugged the wall while Hamish hovered at her bedside as the on-call doctor looked her over. He removed her breathing tube as she was finally breathing on her own and told her to take it slow before speaking. The doctor slipped out of the room leaving Zoey to Hamish and me. As Hamish cooed over Zoey, overjoyed she was all right I stepped out for a moment to call Detective Oscar.

"Detective, good news. Zoey's awake."

"That's wonderful to hear."

"Any news on Catherine yet?" I asked, overly hopeful.

"No, we have a BOLO out for her and I've listed her with missing persons. We're doing everything we can to find her Michael, don't worry." Oscar was trying to sound reassuring, though I could tell he thought the chance of Catherine returning was slim to none. Alec was refusing to talk but that didn't matter, the police had their perp. Even if Alec hadn't signed a full confession, there was plenty of evidence to convict him. He was charged with kidnapping and extortion. With his prior record, he was going back to prison.

The day after my call to Oscar, he showed up at the hospital to see Zoey. He had a couple of routine questions for her before he could officially close his case. He wanted Zoey to confirm, in her own words, that it was Alec who attacked her and that she would testify at Alec's trial. His visit was short and soon he headed out the door and motioned for me to follow him for a quick word.

"Michael, look, I'm sorry but there are no new leads into Catherine's whereabouts. I've done everything I can but with what little Alec has said, I'm afraid we don't have much left to go on. Until someone spots her, there's really nothing we can do. I'm really sorry." Oscar seemed genuinely sincere. He really hoped he could have found Catherine.

"I understand, thanks for everything, John. I appreciate all you've done."

"Look, I know I can't do any more for you but I have a friend who might." Oscar pulled out a card and handed it to me. "He's a P.I. and if anyone can find your girl, he can."

"Thank you." I said as we shook hands. Before he left, the Detective wished me luck. He knew I wouldn't stop searching for Catherine, no matter how long it took. Glancing back at Zoey's hospital room, it was evident that she and Hamish were relieved to be together again. I didn't want to spoil their moment so instead, I went for a walk.

As I made my way through the hospital, I thought about the chain of events that had led me here. I knew Oscar had done everything he could, given the circumstances, but I was left feeling exhausted and alone. I couldn't understand why Catherine hadn't returned yet. What could have happened to her after escaping Alec that would prevent her from coming home? The more days that passed, the more desperate I became for answers. I ventured outside and found a concrete grey bench to sit on. Taking a breath of chilly air, I remembered I was still holding the card from

Oscar. I rang the number and set up a meeting with the P.I. It was all I could think of to do.

I quickly fell into my former routine, but felt like a ghost. Spending my days roaming around the bookshop, helping the one or two customers that would wander in, and evenings spent at The Old Black Curtain, sitting at my usual table. Raymond kept my glass full as I listened to the music, remembering every song Catherine sang. Her replacement was good, but she hardly compared. No one could. A month after Catherine's disappearance, The Old Black Curtain was set to close down. The owner was looking to retire. The thought of not going to the club every night shook me, so I made the old man an offer and bought it from him.

Hamish and I decided to move forward with our expansion plans, opening M&M Tech in Victoria. I told Hamish I would fly out to London and deal with the Board so he could stay with Zoey. After all she had been through, I wasn't about to separate Zoey from her pillar for that length of time. Months passed, and every day the P.I. would update me with his progress, which unfortunately wasn't much.

Hamish and I remained in Victoria with Zoey. We got approval from the Board and were moving forward with M&M Tech., Canada. Zoey, now fully recovered from her physical injuries, was still struggling to move past the ordeal, but she was better. Hamish proposed to her one night at The Old Black Curtain and she delightedly said yes. I was thrilled to see them so happy and starting a life together. All the while, I continued to wait for Catherine. I knew with every passing day and month, she was further away from me. I also knew I was being foolish, waiting for someone who might never come back, but I saw no other option. I began to live in my memories of her, anything to keep her alive. Of course, it really wasn't the same. Even Zoey was different, less bubbly and outgoing. We were all just a little bit less without Catherine.

After seven months of waiting I finally found out what had happened to Catherine. The P.I. had tracked her down to a convent in Kitchener, Ontario. He showed up at the bookshop with a letter addressed to me from Catherine.

My dearest Michael,

This is probably the hardest thing I've ever written. I love you more than words can express. You, Michael, are my soul, my anchor, and I am eternally grateful for your love, for you.

When Alec came to take me, I fought harder than I had ever fought in my life. Unfortunately, it wasn't enough. I blacked out and woke up handcuffed to a bedpost in some small motel room. I tried to escape, but Alec kept me drugged and unconscious most of the time. Then I caught a lucky break. I managed to escape. Only, I had no idea where I was. I wandered around the city, still under the effects of whatever he'd been giving me, and attempted to get my bearings, then I found myself at the bus station. Digging through the pockets of an oversized jacket Alec had put on me earlier, I found his wallet. He always did have more brawn than brains. There was a bit of cash, enough for a ticket, so I bought one and left. I didn't care where the bus was headed. I just had to keep running.

I stayed on the bus 'till the end then hopped on another, paranoid he'd come after me, and too desperate to look back. Eventually, I found myself back in Ontario. I remembered hearing of a convent a couple of hours outside Toronto, so I went there. I just wanted to be safe, feel safe. By the time I got there, though, I had fallen very ill and collapsed as soon as I made it through the main gates. I don't remember much after that. I woke three days later. My plan was to return to you, when I was well enough, but I'm afraid that hasn't happened. I know these last few months must have been horrible for you and I can never make up for that.

There is so much more I wish I had told you. I wish we had a lifetime. But just in case we don't see each other again, there's one last thing I have to tell you. My name, Catherine Miller. I'm sure you've guessed it's not my legal one. It's Eden. Catherine Eden. A girl I walked away from a very long time ago. She was never loved, never accepted, not really. I could see what little kindness I got from the strangers around me for what it really was, pity. That's why I lied. But that name no longer meant anything to me; it was the name of a girl who no longer existed. I loved being your Catherine, she was who I always wanted to be. A strong, self-sufficient woman who worked in a bookstore, sang in a club and loved an earnest man. Everything we shared, Michael, all our precious moments, that was all real. I want you to know that. My foolishness and fear have separated us all these months, but my soul can no longer bear it. The sisters at St. Jude's have been kind and treated me as one of their own, but they are not you. I need you, only you. Please come as soon as you can. I don't know how much longer I have.

All my love,
You're Catherine

I couldn't prevent tears from falling down my cheeks as I absorbed Catherine's letter. My heart was breaking all over again. She had been sick and afraid and I wasn't there for her. Her real name didn't matter, it didn't change my love for her, she would always be Catherine to me. The kindest and most beautiful soul I had ever known.

I pulled myself together and texted Hamish and Zoey with the news. I told them to pack their bags. We were going to bring Catherine home. They were overjoyed that she had been found and said they'd be right over. I packed a small bag and booked three tickets to Toronto. When Hamish and Zoey arrived I called a cab and we were off to the airport within the hour.

The flight felt unbearably long. All we could do was pray there were no delays. During the flight, we speculated on Catherine's well-being and how she'd react when she saw us. While Hamish and Zoey chatted, I attempted to understand the chaos of emotions flowing through me. I was hurt, excited, relieved and worried all at the same time. Zoey was pleased she'd have her maid of honour for the wedding next year after all. She had been putting off wedding plans — the thought of planning her wedding without her best friend was too painful a task, but now everything would be put right again. I felt abandoned, yet also loved. I wondered why she couldn't trust me with the whole truth, why she had felt the need to stay away for so long. But I understood her fear, too. Alec had terrified her and she never had someone she could really trust before, someone she could rely on. But, that is what people do: It's hard, but we lean on each other in times of need, it's how we survive. I would have done anything for her—been anything she needed of me, rather than have her run away. It hurt that she couldn't see that. I had to remind myself that even though it took far longer than I would have liked, eventually she did. She called me her anchor, but really she was mine, the other half of my own soul. Now we would only be complete when together again.

I rented a car at the airport and punched the address for St. Jude's into the GPS. It was a one-and-a-half-hour drive from where we were, two hours if traffic was bad. I drove as quickly as possible while still being safe. It was late by the time we pulled up the convent's drive, the large iron gates already open, ready for us to drive through. Trees lined the dark path, their leaves in different shades of autumn. Even through my desperate need to see Catherine again, I couldn't help but appreciate how beautiful it was here. As we pulled up in front of a large old stone building we saw a small group of nuns standing outside the main doors, waiting for us. I turned off the engine and we climbed out to greet everyone.

"Good evening, you must be Michael?" said one of the nuns, inviting us in. "I'm Sister Rosa. It's lovely to put faces to names. Hamish, Zoey, you are all very welcome. You're all spoken about with great love here."

"Thank you." I replied as I took Sister Rosa's hand in welcome before we all followed her inside out of the cold.

Zoey and Hamish trailed behind a bit as we were led into a small sitting room just off the main entrance. The room was plain and simple, with soft white walls and a large cross hanging above the fireplace. It felt as though we had all stepped back in time. Though the room was pale and minimalist, it gave off a homey feeling of warmth. Zoey and Hamish accepted the offered cups of tea as they sat down on the grey lounge. I was too anxious to sit. As I looked around I couldn't help but notice the sombre atmosphere. Before I could even start to think of why, an old woman came into the sitting room and sat down across from us.

"I am Mother Superior and I'm afraid I have some grievous news for you." Her voice, though soft, was decisive and easily filled the small room.

"Catherine?" I asked, my voice shaking, my thoughts suddenly running wild. I had Hamish in my eye line and could see worry across his face. I watched him gently take Zoey's hand, preparing for the worst, before turning my focus back to Mother Superior.

"Yes. I'm afraid she passed away three days ago."

Her words lingered in the room for several minutes. It took everything in me not to collapse to the floor. Zoey stood from the sofa shaking her head in disbelief for a moment before running out of the room in tears. Hamish shot me a glance before quickly chasing after her. I felt light-headed and shaky.

"Mr. Murphy, please sit down. There is more," Mother Superior said as she gestured to the seat Hamish and Zoey recently occupied. Finally giving way, I slowly sat down as I ran my hands through my hair, my grief almost too thick to see through.

"Mr. Murphy, when Catherine arrived she was already in her second trimester."

"Wait — what?" I asked shocked.

"She was pregnant, Mr. Murphy, about sixteen weeks."

"Pregnant?" I hung my head, trying to make sense of my quickly changing world.

"Yes, you have a beautiful baby girl, Mr. Murphy. Poor Catherine had a rough pregnancy however and took ill throughout. She was quite weak when she went into labour. Catherine died during childbirth."

"A daughter?" I asked, still trying to wrap my head around everything.

"Yes, Mr. Murphy, a beautiful, healthy baby girl. She's perfect, seven pounds, eight ounces." Mother Superior fell silent once more, allowing me to absorb the news. This was all too much. Catherine was gone, but she left a baby behind. My baby.

"Why, why didn't you send for me? Why wait 'till now?" I asked, still trying to sort out what was happening "I should have… I mean, I could have been here, with her… for her."

"Mr. Murphy, we simply followed Catherine's wishes. She did not want you to see her in her weakened state. For months, we continued to ask if she wanted to send for you, but she always declined. She was weak, tired and afraid. Then a few days ago, a private detective showed up. He was persistent in his questioning. He showed us his credentials and identification and explained that you hired him to find Catherine. After he told us that you had sent him, I went to Catherine and let her know he was here. She agreed to speak with him and gave him a letter before sending him away. She told us you would come now, that all of you would. She prayed she'd last long enough to see you. You should know that she spoke about you all every day with the greatest love and admiration; how knowing you had changed her, so profoundly. She was grateful for the time you had together, and the joy she felt having your child. She was an incredible woman and we were all truly blessed to have known her." Mother Superior gave me another moment. This was too much for me, I had held it together up until now but I couldn't keep it together any longer. It took me a good few moments before I could compose myself.

"Can I see her? My little girl?" I finally asked, wiping tears away from my face.

"Sister Mary, would you please?" Mother Superior asked one of the nuns. She promptly left only to return a few moments later with a little newborn in her arms. I stood up from the chaise as Sister Mary placed her in my arms. A little baby with Catherine's eyes and my curly hair, I knew instantly she was ours —Catherine's and mine.

"Does, does she have a name?" I asked

"Catherine named her Elizabeth Vera Murphy, in honour of your aunts, she told us." Mother Superior smiled.

I looked down at my daughter for a long moment, touched by the name Catherine had given her.

"Elizabeth." I smiled at the bundle of joy in my arms. My heart was tearing in two with the death of my soulmate, my Catherine, yet overjoyed at the angel we had created.

I couldn't help but admire the precious, sleeping child in my arms. As I studied Elizabeth, I promised to do right by her and to be thankful for her every day. I couldn't help but think of Catherine and all she would miss. I would give this child everything Catherine couldn't and all the love she was denied when she was small. This tiny angel was now my whole world.

And that my little one is how I found the greatest love of my life and how I found you.

EPILOGUE

Déjà Vu
...16 years later

EVERYTHING LOOKED THE same when I walked in the front door of Betty & Veronica's Books. Zoey left me outside, heading next door to ZZZ's Up Coffee to get us some caffeine. My flight had been long and tiring, much like the whole trip. The only good thing to come from it was running into Thomas again. Though things will never be great between us, it was wonderful to see him doing so well. But I hated being away from my daughter, even knowing that Zoey and Hamish would keep her safe and out of trouble while I was away.

"Birdie upstairs?" Zoey asked, as she came back into the shop, handing me a coffee.

"She should be getting ready to head to The Old Black Curtain," I said, and smiled as I took a sip of the hot black coffee.

"Hamish is already there setting up for the party. Can you believe she's sixteen already?" Zoey asked.

"No," I shook my head, "feels like we only brought her home yesterday," I mused as I heard soft footsteps on the old wooden staircase.

I had a moment of déjà vu, remembering the first time I had walked in and laid eyes on Catherine. Elizabeth slowly came down the wooden staircase with a book in hand. She was beautiful. Petite like her mother, but with my unruly curly hair in a deep shade of auburn; light freckles across her nose and cheeks. She was wearing a light bluish-green knee-length dress bringing out the sparkling hazel in her eyes. Even though Elizabeth had never known her mother, she had an air about her that was so distinctly Catherine. My heart skipped a beat. Every day she reminded me more and more of her mother. I stood, admiring my beautiful daughter as she looked up and smiled.

The End

AUTHOR

 CJ PAXTON WRITES from the heart and for the heart. Her stories illustrates that even the most broken of souls can be mended and find peace.

Originally from Ottawa, Ontario, CJ moved to Victoria, BC with her family in the early 2000s and have lived on the island ever since.

The Old Black Curtain is her second book. Her first, *Choices and Consequences* was published back in 2017 by Tellwell. A story of love and loss, desire and betrayal, and the discovery of how one's actions affect the people we love the most.

CJ's writing reveals her other passion — music. CJ tends to weave her original melodies into her narrative, guiding her characters on their journeys. A recording artist, CJ's first album Anchor My Soul demonstrates the same heart and soul as her stories.

Printed in Canada